WITH

Second
CHANCES

ANNE SCHRAFF

URBAN
UNDERGROUND®

SADDLEBACK
PUBLISHING
www.sdlback.com

© 2013 by Saddleback Educational Publishing

ISBN-13: 978-1-62250-044-4
ISBN-10: 1-62250-044-X
eBook: 978-1-61247-702-7

Printed in Guangzhou, China
NOR/0313/CA21300355

17 16 15 14 13   1 2 3 4 5

CHAPTER ONE

Jaris!" Sereeta screamed, rushing to Jaris's side. Jaris was standing at Harriet Tubman's statue in front of the high school. "Jaris! He's coming!" Sereeta grabbed her boyfriend's hand. "Sunday, he'll be here Sunday!"

Jaris Spain and Sereeta Prince were a couple; both were seventeen-year-old seniors at Tubman.

"Take it easy, babe!" Jaris chuckled. The stream of students going into Harriet Tubman High School barely noticed the excited girl jumping up and down. "What're you saying? Who's coming?"

"My father, Jaris!" Sereeta cried. "Oh, I'm so excited! I haven't seen him since

I was fourteen years old! I've talked to him on the phone, and he e-mails me, but I haven't *seen* him, Jaris, in *three* years!"

"Sereeta," Jaris responded, giving the girl a hug. "I'm so glad for you. That's great!" Jaris knew how hurt Sereeta was when her parents divorced and both of them quickly remarried. They had taken new spouses and made new families, excluding Sereeta from their lives. Sereeta's father had married a woman with two children. He bonded so soon with the little boys that he seemed to have forgotten his daughter.

"Jaris, he's coming on Sunday morning," Sereeta squealed. "He's gonna stay at Grandma's house. He's gonna stay for several days. He called me last night. Oh, Jaris! He wondered if somebody could pick him up. Grandma doesn't like to drive in the heavy traffic around the airport, and her old Volvo has been acting up and …" Sereeta was talking so fast she barely took time for a breath. "Jaris, do you think—"

"Absolutely, babe," Jaris interrupted. "I'll pick him up at the airport. I'll shine up my Ford Focus and pick you up at your grandma's house bright and early. Then we'll go right to the airport and bring your father to your grandma's house."

"Oh, Jaris!" Sereeta cried, hugging him. "I knew you would. I just knew you would. You're amazing, Jare. You're always there for me. Oh, I'm so excited and so nervous. And you should see Grandma! She's beside herself with happiness. She hasn't seen her son in three years either! Jaris, Dad remembers me as a little middle schooler, and now I'm a senior in high school! I hope he even recognizes me!"

"Maybe name tags would be a good idea," Jaris joked, to ease her anxiety.

"Jaris, you wouldn't believe how Grandma's acting," Sereeta confided. "Last night, she was laughing and crying. We were hugging each other and laughing and the tears ran down our faces. Grandma's busy looking up all the foods Dad used to like, the stuff she made for him before he got married. She wants to make his favorite oatmeal bread and those special corn cakes he used to love. She remembers everything, even how he liked his eggs!"

Sami Archer came along. She was a beautiful full-figured girl who was a good friend to Jaris and Sereeta and all their friends. "Hey, look like a party goin' on here, girl," she noted. "What's the scoop, you guys? Somebody win the lottery or somethin'?"

"Oh, Sami," Sereeta cried, "my father is coming on Sunday to visit me and Grandma. We haven't seen him in three years. I'm so excited. Dad sounded as happy to be coming as we're happy to see him. I just can't believe he's finally coming!"

"He say why he's comin' now after all this time?" Sami asked.

"He just said he got to thinking that he needed to come," Sereeta answered. "He said he's been away too long. He's staying for at least three days at Grandma's house.

Oh, Grandma is cleaning like crazy, making everything fresh and nice. She's going after every little cobweb. I remember Dad never cared about the house being perfect. I told Grandma not to worry, but she wants it to look beautiful for him. Grandma said, 'My baby's coming' home, and everything gotta shine!' " Sereeta laughed.

Sereeta had mourned the divorce of her parents when she was in Marian Anderson Middle School. Jaris remembered her spending many lunch hours sitting by herself crying. When Sereeta's father moved away right after the divorce, Sereeta was brokenhearted. Then her mother married Perry Manley, who wasn't happy about having a teenaged girl in the house.

Soon, Sereeta felt as though she had no family at all. Her father had vanished into a new marriage with two stepchildren. Mom was Perry Manley's wife and soon the mother of a baby boy. Sereeta felt like the fifth wheel on the wagon. Her grandmother took Sereeta in to live with her.

"I don't know how I'll concentrate on anything at school, Jaris," Sereeta fretted. "When I think that in three days my father will be here. It's only Thursday, and I gotta go through classes today and tomorrow! Oh, Jaris, I wonder how he'll look. He sent some pictures on the computer, but they weren't good ones. I just can't believe that on Sunday …"

"Just take a deep breath, babe," Jaris instructed her. "Take things an hour at a time. Before you know it, it'll be Sunday morning, and you'll see him coming out of the terminal. It's gonna be great."

A little later, before the first class of the day, Jaris ran into Trevor Jenkins, his best friend. Jaris told him about Sereeta's father coming and how thrilled she was.

"Trevor," Jaris said, "Sereeta's walking on air. She couldn't be happier if she won a million dollars."

Trevor shook his head. "She's not mad at him or anything for staying away so long?" he asked.

"Doesn't seem to be," Jaris replied. "She's just in a state of pure joy."

Two more of Jaris's friends, Kevin Walker and Oliver Randall, got in on the conversation. "Man," Kevin commented, "I wouldn't be so forgiving. I'd hafta say, 'Hey, dude, so you finally decided to drop in and say hello after three years. I'll see if I got time to see you while you're here, but I'm pretty busy. Y'hear what I'm sayin'?' "

Oliver looked thoughtful. His father was a college professor, and his mother was an opera singer. They had an unusual relationship, with his mom traveling a lot. Oliver lived most of the time with his father, but the family always spent summers together. Oliver couldn't imagine not seeing one of his parents for three whole years.

"I kinda agree with Kevin," Oliver noted. "It's kinda bad for a father to not want to see his own daughter for all that time and then to just come popping in. I'm not sure I could just forgive and forget. I sure wouldn't be jumping for joy, I'll tell you that. I gotta admire Sereeta, though. She's a bighearted girl, and she's all ready to welcome the guy with open arms."

"I can't even imagine a dad like that," Jaris agreed. "When I think of my own pop, man, he'd give up his life for Mom and me and Chelsea. I remember when I was in middle school with Sereeta and her father moved away, she was so crushed. I almost hated her father myself for being so cold. But she's so happy right now that I'm glad for her. If she can forgive him and be so happy, I'm gonna do all I can to make it good for her. I'm gonna be at the airport with her to pick the guy up. I want this to be as good as Sereeta thinks it'll be."

On Sunday morning, Jaris got out of bed at four thirty. Mr. Prince's plane was coming in at seven. Jaris had to pick up Sereeta and then make the forty-five-minute drive to the airport. Pop was waiting in the living room when Jaris grabbed his car keys. "Give the little girl a good luck hug for me,

Jaris," Pop told him. "She's gotta be nervous seeing her father after all this time."

"Yeah, Pop, thanks. I will," Jaris responded. It was still dark when Jaris backed out of the driveway. As he drove to Sereeta's house, he thought back to when her father was still around. All he knew about the man was from the few times he'd seen him at Anderson Middle School. Mr. Prince was a big sports fan, and Jaris remembered he was disappointed big-time that Sereeta didn't go out for soccer or volleyball. From what Sereeta told Jaris, Mr. Prince's two boys were very athletic. He was now deeply involved in Little League and other youth sports. Mr. Prince had always wanted sons, and now he had them. He had never seemed comfortable with his little girl.

Jaris rang the doorbell at Sereeta's grandmother's house. Sereeta came to the door, beautiful in a blue pullover and jeans. Jaris kissed her and gave her Pop's good wishes. Grandma Prince was coming down the hall. "I got the guest bedroom all ready," she chirped in a trembling voice. "Oh, I'm so excited! I hope I don't get a heart attack before he comes! I wanna hold my boy in my arms one more time before I leave this earth."

She smiled at Jaris. "Thanks so much for driving Sereeta. I'd be worried sick if she had to drive alone. And I've been havin' dizzy spells that got me worried about going long distances."

"It's my pleasure, Mrs. Prince," Jaris responded. "I'm real happy for both of you. This is a big day."

Jaris and Sereeta walked out to the car.

"Poor Grandma," Sereeta commented. "Half the time she's crying, and half the time she's laughing. She thought about coming with us this morning. Then she said she wanted me to be with my father for a while first, so we can, you know, catch up. Grandma's always looking out for me. She made a meatloaf last night, just how Dad used to like it—onions, green bell peppers, some breadcrumbs, and lotsa beef and pork. Mom was never much for cooking, especially things like meatloaf."

Jaris ached for Sereeta. Her heart was so much into this visit. He hoped only that it would turn out well. If only her father didn't disappoint her as her mother had done so often. Both of them had made her the casualty of their broken marriage. Both of them acted as if, when their marriage ended, their daughter ceased to exist too.

"When I was little," Sereeta remarked as they drove through the darkness, "my father had a paper route. He was just finishing college, and we were short on money. I was about four, and sometimes I rode with him. I'd grab the papers and run them down the driveways. I felt like such a big shot. I loved riding with my dad early in the morning and helping him. Sometimes he'd say I was his little *boy* 'cause I worked with him. That was fun."

"Your parents were real young when they got married, huh, Sereeta?" Jaris asked.

"Yeah." Sereeta nodded. "Grandma was against it. Grandma didn't like my mom. But my parents seemed happy. I don't know if they were or not, but when I was small, they seemed to be. Maybe I was just too dumb to notice stuff going wrong. They stuck it out almost fifteen years, though. I guess they tried."

The traffic got heavier as they neared the airport. A lot of shuttles were on the roads.

"I can't believe that in about an hour I am actually going to see my father again," Sereeta commented. "It's like a dream. I've had so many dreams about him suddenly appearing at our door and me flying into his arms. I've even thought of going where he lives and surprising him. But he, uh, never seemed okay with that, so I didn't."

Sereeta's hands were in her lap, moving constantly. She wore a simple gold bracelet, and she kept turning it around and around. Jaris felt sorry that she was so tense. He thought it shouldn't be that way between a father and his daughter. Jaris thought of his fifteen-year-old sister, Chelsea, and how totally at home she was with Pop. They were so close.

They parked at the airport and went to the terminal where Mr. Prince was arriving. They waited at a large window and watched the large airliners rolling up.

"I've never been on a plane," Sereeta noted. "Oh my gosh, I bet I'd be scared."

"I haven't either," Jaris replied, "but I want to fly. Maybe you and I can take a trip to somewhere cool when we graduate from high school."

"I think that's his flight," Sereeta gasped, grabbing Jaris's hand so tightly that his hand hurt. "I don't see him, though. There are so many passengers!"

"Yeah," Jaris murmured. A horrible thought had occurred to Jaris. What if the guy wasn't on the plane? What if he changed his mind? Sereeta had gone through so many times like that when her mother broke promises. Bitter thoughts moved through Jaris's mind. What kind of a father wouldn't see his kid for three years? Didn't he want to take his sweet girl in his arms and hug her, as Pop hugged Chelsea? There had to be something terribly wrong with the man.

He was worse than Trevor Jenkins's father. Trevor's dad had abandoned his kids too, but he had the excuse of being a hopeless alcoholic. Mr. Prince was a sober, successful man. He had to know how he hurt his daughter by limiting their relationship to a few stinking pictures on the computer and heartless text messages.

"There he is!" Sereeta screamed, running toward a tall man wearing a T-shirt. The front of the shirt read "West Valley Tigers," and the back bore the image of a growling yellow tiger. Jaris saw the man embracing Sereeta, and then they started walking toward Jaris. Jaris stayed back. He didn't want to intrude on the special moment when father and daughter first saw each other.

Mr. Prince was not a handsome man, but he was pleasant looking. He was chunky, but not fat. Jaris could see immediately that Sereeta's stunning beauty came almost entirely from her mother, Olivia.

"Well," Mr. Prince greeted, extending his hand to Jaris, "hello, Jaris Spain. My daughter's told me so much about you, what a marvelous young man you are." He laughed. "I'm not sure you could ever live up to the glowing image she has of you."

Jaris grasped the man's hand. "I think the world of Sereeta," he responded. "Nice to meet you, Mr. Prince."

Jaris picked up Mr. Prince's two bags. The father walked with his arm around Sereeta's shoulders. Jaris stayed a little behind Sereeta and her father. He didn't want to take anything away from these moments.

"We should have done this a long time ago," he declared. "Where did the time go?"

In the parking garage, Jaris loaded the two bags into his trunk. Mr. Prince placed his hands on his daughter's shoulders and held her at arm's length.

"You are absolutely beautiful, Sereeta. The pictures you've posted didn't do you justice," Mr. Prince remarked.

"Thanks, Dad," Sereeta responded. "I'm *so glad* you're here. Grandma is beside herself with excitement too. She made your favorite meatloaf and the string beans you liked and even your sweet potato pie!"

"Oh, my!" Mr. Prince replied, patting his spreading waistline. "I don't eat that kind of stuff much anymore. My wife is always after me to eat salads, lean meat, fish, stuff like that. I try to get a lot of exercise. I coach my sons' Little League team. As you can see, they play for the West Valley Tigers. I get a lot of exercise coaching my boys. Still, every time I cheat and have a supersized burger, the old pounds hop back on."

Jaris winced when Mr. Prince said "my sons" and "my boys." Sereeta had said he was very close to his stepsons. That was well and good, but what about his daughter? Jaris fought the resentment rising within him. The guy rubbed Jaris the wrong way.

Sereeta and her father sat together in the backseat as Jaris took the wheel for the ride to her grandmother's house. As Mr. Prince got into the car, Jaris noticed that the names "Donovan" and "Kyle" were on his T-shirt too. The stepsons.

"What took me so long to do this?" Mr. Prince lamented.

"I don't know, Dad, but I'm sure glad you're finally here," Sereeta said.

"Life gets in the way," the man remarked wistfully. "My job, going here and there, seminars, meetings. The weeks whipped by, turned into months. And Little League. It's great, but it takes a lot of time. It's a big commitment. The boys are always practicing, playing. My wife laughs and says we're actually driving our kids around more than we're doing anything else. But the payoff comes when they win a game."

Mr. Prince's face broke into a big smile. "Donovan," he went on, "my oldest boy, he's eleven. He's a pitcher. This kid is something else. I thought I was tall. I'm just about six feet, but this kid is already five eleven! And Kyle, my youngest, he's ten. He's an outfielder. When they're together in a game, they just dominate."

Jaris's hands tightened on the steering wheel. What had begun as a mild dislike for Mr. Prince was rapidly turning into hatred. He'd been gone from his daughter, his only biological child, for three years. He'd been living with these stepkids. Now was not the time to be talking about them. Now was the time to reconnect with his daughter.

"You always did love sports, Dad," Sereeta murmured. Jaris noticed that her voice was slightly forlorn, and that hurt him.

"Yeah, especially baseball," the man continued, oblivious to Sereeta's feelings. "Football's good too, but baseball's my game. Donovan is such a big boy, though, he can't decide what to concentrate on.

He's a double-threat athlete. He could probably make it as a great quarterback in high school, but I'm not keen on my boy playing football. Too many injuries in that sport. I'd rather he stick with baseball."

Mr. Prince was smiling broadly. "Now Kyle is even a little bigger, weight-wise. We might not be able to stop him from going out for football. He loves the game. He's a Raiders fan."

The sun was up now, and traffic was heavier than before. Jaris had a headache. He usually didn't get headaches except when he was angry, and he was very angry with Sereeta's father. But there was nothing he could do about it. If he told Mr. Prince what he really thought, he would just sour the long awaited visit. In the end, Sereeta would be the one hurt. So Jaris just sat grimly at the wheel, glaring occasionally into his rearview mirror at the insensitive fool. He was still rambling on about his stepkids while Sereeta sat there looking sad. He hadn't yet bothered to ask Sereeta anything about what was going on in her life, what she liked, how she felt.

Even as they neared Grandma's house, Mr. Prince was still blowing about the step-kids. "Of course, the big dream is getting to Williamsport, Pennsylvania. The Little League World Series. Donovan just turned eleven, so he's got one more shot at it. Kyle has more time to be part of a championship team." He paused then and asked, "Jaris, you're a big, athletic looking guy. What sports do you go out for?"

"I hate sports," Jaris answered with raw bitterness. It wasn't true. He enjoyed playing basketball with his friends, and he loved to run. He liked to watch football and baseball, and in middle school he played soccer. But he was infuriated by how this guy was raving about his stepsons' accomplishments and ignoring Sereeta and her life. He just blurted out his response.

"Oh, that's too bad," Mr. Prince commented. "Sports are one of life's most enjoyable activities. I find they build character too, especially in young men."

Finally, Jaris pulled into the driveway of Grandma Prince's home. Mrs. Prince was outside in the front yard, waiting for them. She'd seen the car coming all the way from the corner. She was flushed with excitement. She had arthritic legs, but she almost ran toward the car. "Bubba!" she screamed, using the pet name for her son from his teenaged years. "Bubba!"

Mr. Prince got out of the car. His mother reached him and threw her arms around him, tears running down her face. The son stood there, arms hanging at his sides. Then, almost as an afterthought, he kissed his mother.

"I'm not Bubba anymore, Mom," he corrected her. He seemed embarrassed.

CHAPTER TWO

Jaris made eye contact with Sereeta. Still sitting in the car, they were so close they didn't need words to say what they were both thinking about this man.

Jaris said softly, "Call you later."

Sereeta mouthed the words, "Love you," and got out of the car.

As Jaris backed out of the driveway, he felt sick to his stomach. He tried to tell himself things would get better from now on. The guy would stop bragging about his stepsons. He would start asking Sereeta about her life. He would actually listen with interest when she told him. Jaris tried to tell himself that, but he couldn't convince himself. The guy was a jerk. Only a jerk would voluntarily absent himself from his child's life for three years, as Mr. Prince did.

When Jaris got home, Pop was outside in the front yard, trying to coax life back into a small tree Mom had planted. It was a jacaranda, Mom's favorite tree, and it was turning yellow. Pop was feeding it from a plant food bottle. When Jaris got out of the car, Pop looked up.

"How'd it go, Jaris?" Pop asked. One look at Jaris's face was answer enough. "That bad, huh?"

"Pop, did you know this Prince dude back when they lived around here, when he was married to Sereeta's mom?" Jaris asked. "I mean, was he *always* a jerk?"

Pop shrugged. "Monie hung out with Olivia a lot, and we saw a lotta Sereeta. But he'd usually be home watchin' sports on TV. He's a jock. Sports is his religion, y'hear what I'm sayin'? So what happened?"

"He gets in the car with Sereeta," Jaris started to explain, "and the whole time he's bragging about his stepsons, what great baseball players they are. I mean, he's goin' nonstop. He hasn't seen Sereeta in three years, and he can't even ask her about school, her activities, what's going on in her life. Nothing."

Jaris jammed his keys into his jeans' pocket and shook his head sadly. "I coulda strangled the jerk. The whole time I was burning mad. I mean, Sereeta was in that play with me, *A Tale of Two Cities*. She's taking AP American History, and she's got an A-plus average. Didn't he want to hear about any of that? I felt like screaming. Oh man, I got a headache, Pop."

Mom stepped outside. "I couldn't help overhearing. It wasn't good, huh?" she noted sadly. "I was afraid it wouldn't be."

"Sereeta's father is a creep," Jaris snarled.

Mom sighed. "Well, we shouldn't be surprised I guess," she suggested. "When he and Olivia got divorced, he didn't ask for any set visitation. He just moved away.

A lot of divorced fathers stay close to the kids. But at least he came now, Jaris. That's a plus. Anything Sereeta gets from him is a plus."

"I don't know, Mom," Jaris objected. "Sereeta's in a pretty good place right now. I think it would have been better if he'd never come at all, instead of coming and rubbing her face in his wonderful stepsons all the time. What's wrong with a guy like that? I felt like tellin' him, 'Stuff it, jerk.' But I couldn't do that without hurting Sereeta."

Sereeta's father planned to stay for two days, Sunday and Monday. Before he came, he was talking about three or four days, but now it was down to two. Monday was a school holiday for the kids, a teacher enrichment day. But regular classes resumed on Tuesday. Sereeta would be back in school among her friends. Jaris hoped she wouldn't be too emotionally ragged by then. He hoped her father would eventually remember that she was his child and give her a chance to bond with him.

On that Sunday afternoon, Jaris went to a car show with Kevin Walker, who'd come from Texas last year. Jaris was still griping about Sereeta's father while driving to the show. Kevin just shook his head.

"I guess she'd be better off not having a father at all," Kevin remarked. "I have some real faint good memories of my dad, about riding on his shoulders at the park. But then he disappeared into prison, and he died. I never really missed him. Now with my mom, that was different. I miss her every day. She was a great mom."

Kevin smiled weakly as he remembered his mother. "Then she got sick, and they said there was nothing they could do for her anymore. When the hospice nurse came, I wanted to die. I wanted to curl up on the floor and die. I felt so bleak. But my grandparents, they've been wonderful. Even when Mom was alive, they were there, going on vacations with us. I guess I'm lucky. I had a good Mom until I was fifteen and now I got really cool grandparents."

"Sereeta has a nice grandmother," Jaris noted. "But her parents—her mom and dad—are not really there for her, that's the tough part. I bet that jerk Prince is over there now, breaking his mom's heart too. She came running to meet him, and he stood there like a stick when she was hugging him. She called him 'Bubba'—I guess that's a pet name from way back—and he acts real embarrassed. I'm telling you, Kevin, he's a first-class creep."

"I think the world has more creeps than good people, Jaris," Kevin commented.

"No, I don't think so. Maybe it's fifty-fifty," Jaris quipped.

At the car show, all the new models were on display on moving platforms, with beautiful girls standing near them.

"Someday I'm gonna get one of those," Kevin declared.

"A Porsche?" Jaris asked.

"Yeah. I'm gonna get me a Porsche," Kevin said.

"I don't think I'll ever be rich enough for one of those babies," Jaris remarked.

"I'm gonna be a teacher, but teachers don't make a fortune."

Kevin laughed. "You wanna be like Mr. Pippin? Dude, I'd rather be dead!"

Jaris laughed too. "No, I'm gonna have fun teaching. I'll be like Ms. McDowell or maybe even Mr. Myers. I want to write too, and maybe I'll get a novel done and be famous. Maybe I'll win the Pulitzer Prize, man. I saw in the window of the English department office that there's a short story contest for seniors here at Tubman. Maybe I'll enter that, get my writing career off the ground."

Jaris was half laughing as he spoke. "There's three nice prizes and trophies. Third place gets two hundred fifty, second place five hundred, and the top prize is a thousand. I'm not good enough for the top prize, but maybe I could come in third. I'm gonna enter that contest."

"Lydell is entering too," Kevin responded. "Ever since Mr. Myers praised that diary he's been writing in, Lydell's like a new person. He's got hope now."

"That's good," Jaris said. Lydell Nelson was a total loner since his freshman year, just sitting alone and writing in his journal. A lot of the kids were afraid of him. But Kevin befriended him and brought him out of his shell.

"You been writing short stories, Jaris?" Kevin asked.

"A few, but they were junky," Jaris answered. "I tossed them. But I'm getting better, I think. Who knows? Hey, Kevin, what're you gonna do to be able to afford a Porsche?"

"I haven't figured that one out yet," Kevin replied. "The dude down at the gym said I box pretty good, but the fight game is on the skids. Used to be the heavyweight champ was famous. Everybody knew his name. Now most people can't even name him. I'm a good runner, but there's no money in that. Even if I'd get to the Olympics and win a medal, who cares? The medals aren't worth anything. A few dudes get famous and get their mugs on cereal boxes, but most Olympic winners just disappear without a trace. I was reading about this Wilma Rudolph. She was fantastic. Cute too. But she spent most of the rest of her life scrounging around in menial jobs. I don't know. Maybe I'll have to …" A wicked smile came to Kevin's face.

"What?" Jaris pressed him.

"Oh man, I don't know," he shrugged. "I know one thing. I'm not sitting through four years of college, I'll tell you that. I'm not smart enough to snag a good career like engineering. I gamble sometimes. I'm not supposed to at my age, but my friends do it for me. I won a coupla times on the ponies. I got two hundred bucks on one race when my old long-shot nag came stumbling in."

"You can't make a living betting on horses," Jaris remarked.

"I don't want to just make a living, man," Kevin protested. "I want something real good. I wanna take Carissa for a ride in my Porsche. I'm willing to do most any-thing to get my hands on real money. Man,

my grandparents are in that old house, dod-
dering around, saving coins in the cookie
jar. Grandma goes, 'Whoopee, Roy, we got
ten dollars in the jar now! That do add up.'
And Grandpa goes, 'Lena, you always was
good with money.' "

A concerned look came over Kevin's
face. "Last month," he continued, "the
hot water heater got busted, and they
didn't have enough money to fix it. I
didn't mind the cold showers, but they're
old and they got aches and pains. They
need hot water. They oughtn't be suf-
fering like that. We got it fixed now. I
kicked in some money from that lousy
pizza job I got. Business is really down
there. Our tips are down. I need to make
some real money, Jare."

Jaris reached over and grabbed Kevin's
forearm. "Kevin, do you know what it
would do to your grandparents if you did
something stupid to get your hands on
some fast money?" Jaris asked. "You got
any idea what that would do to them?"

Kevin's expression darkened. "Don't worry about me, dude," he said darkly.

"Well, don't talk stupid and make me worry," Jaris ordered him. "We haven't known each other that long, Kevin, but you're my friend. I like you. I want us guys—Trevor, Derrick, Oliver, you, and me—to visit Tubman High ten years from now. We'll go down the trail under the eucalyptus trees and tell those guys who'll be sitting there then that we made it. We'll tell 'em we have good lives now, and we made it. I want us *all* to still be friends. I don't want to lose one of my homies."

Kevin laughed. "You're a pretty arrogant dude, Jaris," he chuckled. "You think you can change the world."

"You better believe it," Jaris asserted.

"I'm goin' over there and asking that chick in the short shorts if I can sit at the wheel of the Porsche," Kevin announced. "I'm gonna tell her I'm a rock idol, and I'm considering buying a Porsche."

Kevin walked up to the girl, and, within minutes, he was sitting at the wheel of the Porsche, grinning out the window at Jaris.

Back home, around three in the afternoon, Jaris called Sereeta. "Hey, how's it goin', babe?" he asked her.

"Everything's fine," Sereeta replied. "We're all going to dinner at Ye Olde Boathouse, that nice place on the bay. My father is taking Grandma and me. You've been there, huh, Jaris?"

"Yeah, it's a good place," Jaris responded. He wanted to ask her if the jerk was still going on about his stepsons and their athletic triumphs. But he knew that would be out of line. "Okay, babe. Call me anytime, okay? I mean if you get tired of hearing about the Little League, babe, call me. I'll climb on my steed and rescue you."

Sereeta laughed. "That's nice to know."

Pop looked up from the newspaper. "She okay?" he asked.

"Yeah, she seems to be. They're going to dinner at Ye Olde Boathouse," Jaris answered.

"Poor kid!" Pop remarked, shaking his head. "She struck out with both parents. Tough. She's battin' zero. But I gotta take my hat off to her. She's a great girl, full of smarts and energy, and she's got a good heart. She's doin' okay."

"But it has to have left its mark on her," Mom commented. "Our psychological health is built on the loving relationships we've had, just as our physical health depends on getting nutritious food."

Jaris didn't like to hear Mom talking like that. Pretty soon she'd be on the line to Grandma Jessie again. Mom often told her own mother about things going on in the Spain household.

"Like Pop says," Jaris affirmed, "Sereeta is doing fine. She can handle it."

"Yeah," Pop chimed in, "some of these little hothouse flowers, they got their parents givin' 'em everything, fawnin' over

34

them, making excuses for all the rotten things they do. They don't always do so good. When they get in the real world, they fall apart when the least little trouble comes along. That's why I believe in comin' down hard on my kids when they cross the line. Which reminds me, is Chelsea still sittin' out there on the curb with that little punk?"

Jaris looked out the window. "Yeah, Chelsea and Heston are sitting there," he reported.

"They been there for like six hours," Pop remarked. "What they got to say that they need six hours to say it?"

"Lorenzo," Mom chided, "Heston just got to the house about thirty minutes ago."

"Nah, it's been longer 'n that," Pop insisted. "He ain't got his hands all over her, has he?" Pop got up from his chair and headed to the window. "Heston is okay as punks go, but I don't trust any of 'em. Girls get too chummy with these grabby punks. Before you know it, she turns out like Rahleen Halliday with the reputation of a trashy chick. So many guys pawing over Rahleen, she got to be wore out." Pop walked toward the door.

"Lorenzo!" Mom scolded. "Don't embarrass Chelsea again."

"Oh, hey!" Pop said with a phony hurt look on his face. "Would I do such a thing?"

Pop walked to the curb and spoke to his daughter. "Hey, little girl, you and Heston havin' a nice conversation out here? You maybe talkin' about the political situation in Washington? That guy up there in the White House, he's got his work cut out for him. I bet he never thought this job would be so tough, huh?"

"We were talking about school, Pop," Chelsea answered. "That Mr. Tidwell is so hard. Heston doesn't mind him 'cause he's better in math than me, but I really am glad Shadrach is tutoring me. Otherwise, I'd be doomed."

"Well, little girl, you got that B on your last test, and I'm proud of you for that," Pop told her. "You gotta know some math in this world, or you can't even figure out the grocery bill, y'know what I'm sayin'?"

Pop turned his attention to Heston. "So, little man, those were nice tops you got Chelsea for her birthday, one of them kinda low cut, but not too bad. Coulda been worse. So how you doin' in school, Heston?"

"Very good, sir," Heston replied. "I have an A average."

"Wow!" Pop exclaimed. "That's real good. The other day I was there at the Holiness Awakening Church with Pastor Bromley. I seen you and your family there. Real fine to see a guy your age with your family listening to Pastor Bromley. He's kinda long-winded sometimes. I seen some elderly lady fallin' asleep, but the pastor has good stuff to say. Can't go wrong doing what he says. Seems like you got good parents there, Heston. They were sittin' there singin' up a storm. That's one of my favorites. A good rousin' hymn. Just what we need when we been listenin' to Pastor Bromley for a while."

Pop stopped for a moment to snicker. "I seen this fella once, he been sittin' there so long listenin' to the pastor, that his leg was sleepin'. Up he gets and nearly tumbles over when his leg don't work. But Lonnie Archer caught him before he went down hard."

Pop turned and headed back into the house, still chuckling. Heston looked at Chelsea, not sure of what to make of her father. Chelsea giggled as Pop walked back to the house.

Later that same day, Jaris was on his computer working on his short story for the contest when his phone rang. It was six thirty.

"Hi, Jaris," Sereeta said. "You busy?" She didn't sound right. Jaris sat up straight, his heart pounding.

"Never too busy for you. Wassup, babe?" Jaris asked.

"My father contacted some of his old buddies in the neighborhood," Sereeta explained in a forlorn voice. "They all decided to go see the baseball game tonight. Grandma's tired from all the excitement, and she's turning in early. So I'm free if you feel like riding your steed over here and hanging for a while."

"You got it, babe," Jaris told her. "I'll be there as soon as I get saddled up."

Jaris drove to Sereeta's grandmother's house and picked her up. Amateur astronomers were set up in the park with their telescopes. People could take turns looking at the rings of Saturn and other beautiful night sky wonders. Jaris suggested checking it out. Sereeta thought that would be fun, and they ended up looking through the telescopes. On the way home, they stopped for lattes.

Sitting at a table in the coffee shop, Sereeta started explaining what happened after Jaris dropped her and her father at the house. "Dad got kinda bored and wanted to spend some time with some of the guys he knew from the neighborhood. He went with Guthrie Shaw, Derrick's father, and Lonnie Archer, Sami's dad. Dad said he wanted to tell them about his boys and all they're doing." Sereeta's voice trailed off.

When Sereeta turned and looked at Jaris, she had tears in her eyes.

"I'm sorry, babe," Jaris sympathized.

"It's okay," Sereeta shrugged. "Really it is. He's so happy now. My father is really happy. His wife's first husband—the father of those boys—he let my dad adopt them. My father adopted Donovan and Kyle. I never knew that until today. They got his last name. I guess my dad was really un-happy with my mom for a lotta years, and I … I was part of that. I mean, I was this kid from a really bad, unhappy marriage. I'm almost like the yucky furniture from the first apartment that you always hated. You don't want to take it with you to the next place."

"Sereeta," Jaris asserted, "you're his daughter, and you're a treasure. He should see that."

Sereeta smiled and resolutely wiped her eyes. "I don't know what I'd do without you, Sir Jaris," Sereeta sniffed, trying to smile.

CHAPTER THREE

Earlier that evening, Sereeta's father had climbed into Guthrie Shaw's van, and the three men headed for the baseball park. When Mr. Prince was married to Olivia, he and Lonnie Archer and Guthrie Shaw often went to games together. Mr. Prince remembered his friends bragging about their kids' athletic skills, and he felt left out with no son to talk about. It was different now. He couldn't wait to tell his old friends about Donovan and Kyle Prince.

"So, Guthrie," Mr. Prince asked, "how's your boy, Bruce, doing now in sports?"

"He's playing football and he's great," Guthrie answered proudly. "I think that boy might end up bein' a pro."

"My oldest boy, Donovan, he's a wonder," Mr. Prince stated, smiling widely. "He's an all-star now. He's taller than I was at that age. And what a slugger!"

"My nephew, Leon, he's only eleven," Lonnie Archer chimed in, "but he's doing fine in Little League. His team might win the regionals, and it won't be hap'nin' without him. Maya's doing well on the softball team. Wow! You should see how she slugs that ball."

"My youngest boy, Kyle, he's ten," Sereeta's father said. "He's in Little League too, and I hope he sticks with baseball. We're afraid he might switch to football."

The men bought hot dogs and sodas and headed for their seats in the stadium.

"You know, man," Guthrie Shaw said, "your daughter, Sereeta, she's quite a girl too. My oldest son, Derrick, says everybody just loves her. She's as beautiful on the inside as she is on the outside. I bet you're real proud of her too."

"Yes, indeed," Mr. Prince agreed.

"I bet you guys are havin' quite a time getting caught up on everything," Lonnie Archer said. "I was surprised you called me to come to the game. I didn't think you'd want to spend time with us when you haven't seen your girl in some time. My daughter, Sami, she's real close with Sereeta."

"Well, Sereeta wanted to see her boyfriend," Mr. Prince lied. "So I thought I'd have a night out with my old pals."

One of the players on the field hit a home run, and the bleachers went wild. Sereeta's father cried, "That kid who just hit the home run reminds me of my boy Donovan. He's got the same moves. Donny hit a homer in a really crucial game last year. It was the winning hit."

"It'd been nice if Sereeta and Jaris woulda come along with us tonight," Lonnie Archer suggested.

"Oh, Jaris told me he hates sports," Mr. Prince replied.

"No way!" Guthrie Shaw protested. "The boy's on the track team. Plus he goes to the baseball and football games with Sereeta sometimes. I seen him with his pop at a lot of Tubman games too. Jaris is cheerin' with the best of them."

After the game, as the three men rode home, Lonnie Archer turned to Sereeta's father. "Dude," he began, "we go back a long way. I wanna ask you somethin', but I don't want to offend you in no way. It's just somethin' been bothering me for a good long while. I got a daughter same age as Sereeta, my Sami. Now me and Mattie, we been on the outs with each other a few times, but we're still together. But if we'd of split up, I woulda walked through fire and water to be with my girls at least once a week. Sereeta been tellin' Sami how much she's missed you all this time."

Lonnie was anxious about asking his question, but he had to know. "I'm just curious. Why'd you stay away for so long? Sereeta needed a daddy real bad when her mother got sick and all."

Mr. Prince looked uncomfortable. "I have been incredibly busy," he insisted. "When I got remarried, I had a new wife and two little boys who needed a father. Their own father was out of the picture almost since they were born. That man was very happy when I adopted his sons. He was glad to be relieved of the burden. Here I was with a nine-year-old boy and a seven-year-old, and they needed a father desperately."

Lonnie and Guthrie were listening intently. "And then," Prince went on, "well, … my ex-wife, Olivia, I thought she could adequately care for Sereeta. I helped financially, of course, and I always sent Sereeta e-mails and text messages. You know, I thought it was just better that I focus on my boys and let Olivia … you know … take over there."

"But Sereeta been goin' through some hard times with her mother being sick and all," Guthrie Shaw told him. "Poor little girl been like a lost soul. If it hadn't been for her friends—Jaris, of course, Alonee Lennox, Lonnie's Sami, and the others—I'm not sure that child would have survived. I'm not judgin' you, man, but I'm just wonderin.'"

Anger came into Mr. Prince's eyes. "Yes, you *are* judging me, Guthrie. And you too, Lonnie," he growled. "And I don't think it's fair of you. My ex-wife had custody of Sereeta, and I wasn't aware of any problems. Everything seemed to be just fine. I was … uh … never as comfortable being the father of Sereeta as I am with my boys. Girls are so different. A father can't really … bond with a girl like he can with a boy. I thought I was doing what was best for Sereeta. She seems like a very happy, well-adjusted girl now, and we are enjoying our visit very much. I hope to come more often now. But whatever happens, I think I made the right decision."

The rest of the ride home was silent.

After Guthrie Shaw dropped Mr. Prince off at his mother's house, the two men talked about what had happened.

"That's one cold dude," Guthrie remarked with a shudder.

"You got that right," Lonnie Archer agreed. "Y'hear him all durin' the game? He had nothin' to say about Sereeta, just about those stepsons of his. He ain't seen Sereeta in years. You'd think he'd be talkin' about all the stuff she's been doin', what a smart girl she is. It's like the sun rises and sets on Donovan and Kyle, and the poor little girl sits in the dark."

"Saddest thing I ever seen," Guthrie Shaw commented.

"My little girl Sami," Lonnie Archer said, "she's been telling me for years how it's been so long since Sereeta seen her father that she's almost forgot what the man looks like. Right after the divorce, Sereeta was always lookin' sad, like a little lost sheep. She didn't think her dad would move out of town on top o' that."

"You think what we said made him feel guilty?" Guthrie Shaw asked.

"I'd like to think so, but probably not," Lonnie Archer replied.

Later that night, Jaris dropped Sereeta home at about ten o'clock. She walked into the house to find her grandmother had gone to bed. Her father was sitting on the couch watching the news.

"Was it a good game, Dad?" Sereeta asked him.

"Yeah, three homers," Mr. Prince answered. "You should've come along, Sereeta. I'm here only two days. We need to spend as much time together as we can."

Her father's comment puzzled Sereeta. She hadn't been invited.

"Jaris and I went down to the park where the amateur astronomers were looking at the planets on their telescopes," she responded. "They let anybody look in the telescopes too. It's cool."

Mr. Prince looked at his daughter, and Sereeta looked back at him. Both of them seemed uncomfortable. They were like strangers meeting for the second time in the same day and not knowing what more to say to each other. They had used up their few words of conversation, and now they were almost frantic. Sereeta finally broke the awkward silence. "Goodnight, Dad," she said.

"Sereeta," Lester Prince asked suddenly, "you're happy, aren't you?"

Sereeta stopped. "Sure," she replied.

"I thought so," he said quietly. "You have a nice boyfriend and a lot of friends. I guess you got it made. Doing well in school. Like they say, everything coming up roses."

Sereeta smiled at her father, not understanding why he was talking this way. She turned to go to her room.

Lester Prince smiled nervously. He watched the beautiful young woman disappear down the hall. He didn't enjoy being with her. Strange, he felt so comfortable with Donovan and Kyle, roughhousing and talking about sports. Sereeta was his daughter, but he was eager for the visit to be over. He was glad day one was over, and now there was just one more day to get through. Then he'd be back on the plane going home. He thought he'd send for the shuttle. He didn't want Sereeta and Jaris to take him to the airport. He would have to endure some emotional farewell. Anyway, Lester Prince got the distinct feeling that Jaris Spain didn't like him.

The father realized today, more than ever, how much the girl looked like her mother. They were both so beautiful. His new wife was attractive but not beautiful. All the sad memories of his first marriage swept over the man, filling him with sorrow. Seeing Sereeta's haunting beauty brought back his experience with Olivia, his ex-wife.

Lester Prince remembered how he had loved Olivia and how he had fought with his mother over marrying her. Once married, what a disaster his efforts turned out to be. He'd tried but failed to meet the needs of his fragile young wife. Olivia always believed he didn't really love her. Once she accused him of being unable to love. He thought maybe she was right in a way. He couldn't love as unconditionally as she wanted him to do. His new wife was pleasant and uncomplicated. When Lester Prince looked at his stepsons, he saw his wife's sweet, calm nature.

When Mr. Prince looked at Sereeta, he saw Olivia and reacted as he did to his ex-wife. His feelings were no one's fault. Olivia had felt unloved, and he had felt incapable of meeting her needs. In the end, the marriage collapsed under the weight of their mutual unhappiness. Even before the divorce, Lester Prince had known his second wife, Evie, a secretary in an office he frequently visited. They had exchanged pleasantries, and they were attracted to each other. She'd been married and divorced, and she was a single mother of two boys. Knowing her made it easier to get his divorce. He had something to look forward to, the prospect of a second chance at happiness.

Lester Prince moved far from the scene of his unhappy marriage. He quickly married Evie, and her boys filled his life. They were wildly funny, rambunctious boys, who needed only footballs and baseballs to be happy. Marrying Evie was like walking from a dark place into the sunlight.

He had dreaded this visit with his mother and Sereeta. The obligation preyed on his conscience, but he kept putting it off. He knew he should visit them. It was the right thing to do. But postponing the trip was the appealing and easy thing to do. He kept thinking that, if he waited a little longer, the baggage of his sad past would weigh less heavily on him. But just looking at Sereeta made the baggage heavier, not lighter.

The thought of getting through tomorrow was unbearable.

At eleven thirty, Lester Prince went to his mother's room to awaken her. But she was lying there, her eyes wide open. "Ma," he whispered, "I just got a call from my office. I gotta get back right now. Big project coming up, and I'm the only one can handle it. I'm calling the shuttle."

"What?" the old woman gasped.

"Tell Sereeta for me," he said hoarsely. "Give her my love. I'll come back to visit soon." He knew that was a lie. Bessie knew it was a lie. But he had to say it. He called the shuttle and carried his bags down the driveway. He went outside and waited in the darkness until the shuttle pulled up. He fled into the shuttle as the driver loaded his bags.

As the vehicle backed out the driveway, Lester Prince heaved a sigh of relief. He glanced out thankfully as they reached the main highway and headed for the freeway ramp. He was escaping, just as he did that last time almost three years ago, when he and Olivia had had their final fight. Her screams had rung in his ears as he fled into the night. The lawyers handled the divorce.

He never saw Olivia Prince again. He didn't want to.

Back at Sereeta's house, Bessie Prince sighed and picked herself up from her bed. She felt very weary but not tired. When her son told her he had to go, she knew he did—but not because of business. She put on her robe and slippers, and she shuffled down the hallway to the phone in the living room. She dialed Jaris's cell phone number.

"Jaris?" she said when he answered.

"Huh? Wh—" Jaris mumbled. Then, becoming fully awake, he asked, "Is this Sereeta's grandma?"

"Yes," Bessie Prince replied. "I need to tell you that Sereeta's father just left. He made some excuse about his work, but I know he just didn't wanna stay no more. Sereeta's sleepin' now. She's all right. But she's gonna need you in the morning. Can you come over then, boy? It'd be an awful big help."

"Yes," Jaris agreed quickly. "I'll be there first thing in the morning. There's no school at Tubman tomorrow. I'll be there around seven. I'll eat breakfast with you folks."

"Bless your heart, boy," the grandmother told him. "I'll make a nice breakfast for us all. It'll help."

"Thanks for letting me know," Jaris said. Ending the call, he fell back on his pillow, his eyes wide and staring. He didn't sleep for the rest of the night.

Jaris was out of bed by six in the morning. Pop appeared in the hallway outside the bathroom. "Wassup, boy?" he asked.

"Pop, Sereeta's father split last night," Jaris explained. "He was gonna stay two days, but he just left. Sereeta's grandmother called me and asked if I'd come over to help Sereeta get through this. So I'm going over there."

"Why the lousy freakin' creep," Pop snarled.

Mom appeared in her robe. "What's going on? What's all the yelling about?"

"That freakin' Prince dude up and left last night," Pop responded. "Poor little Sereeta all upset. Whatta bum! Jaris wants to go over there and be with Sereeta and her grandma. But, hey, I got a better idea. I'm goin' with ya, boy. That poor old grandma sure ain't up to cookin' no breakfast. I'll load up the pancake stuff, the syrup, butter, some nice pork sausages, eggs, and I'll make a nice breakfast." Pop looked at Mom, expecting an argument.

"That's a good idea," Mom remarked. "I'll go too. I'll get Chelsea up right now."

The Spains dressed and loaded the food into Jaris's Ford. They arrived at about quarter to seven. Jaris rang the doorbell, and Sereeta's grandmother answered. Sereeta was sitting at the kitchen table, drinking coffee.

"Mr. Spain and Mrs. Spain, Jaris and little Chelsea!" Bessie Prince cried out. "They all come, Sereeta. They all come, baby."

"We brought breakfast fixin's," Pop declared. "I'm goin' to the kitchen right now and get everything goin'. Times like this, we gotta stick together. Sereeta, don't be sad, little girl. You got family right here. You better believe it. I'll get breakfast on the table in no time, Bessie. I'm a pretty good cook."

Pop stopped on his way to the kitchen and grabbed the girl for a big hug. He winked at her and promised, "You got a treat comin', little girl. Gonna be *some* breakfast."

Then Mom went over and hugged Sereeta, followed by Chelsea. Jaris was last to embrace Sereeta and gave her a big kiss.

When the Spains had come marching in, Sereeta'd looked shocked. Now a smile trembled on her lips. Mom sat with her at the kitchen table. "Sereeta," Mom stated, "I've known you since you were born. Me and your mom used to take you and Jaris to the park together. You're practically my little girl too. When either of us wanted a night out, your mom would babysit Jaris, and we'd babysit you."

"Yeah!" Pop shouted from the kitchen. "I used to take you for piggyback rides around the park. Knowin' you and what fun a little girl was, me and Monie wanted a girl of our own. So when Chelsea come, we were in heaven."

"Remember, Sereeta," Chelsea added, "you taught me how to ride a two-wheel bike. I thought I couldn't do it, and you kept running alongside me and saying, 'You can do it, you can do it.' Finally I did, and you cheered."

"You guys," Sereeta sighed.

Soon the little house was filled with the aroma of pancakes and pork sausages. Mom and Chelsea set the table, and Pop and Jaris carried in the food.

Grandma Prince tried to help, but Pop ordered, "Sit right down at the table, Bessie. You work hard enough. Time somebody waited on you."

"Oh, what a beautiful breakfast!" Sereeta's grandmother gasped.

Pop looked at Sereeta and said, "Lissen up, little girl. We're your family. This right here, this is your family. Jaris and me, Monie here, Chelsea. You're in our family tree, little girl, and you're never gonna fall out."

CHAPTER FOUR

When Jaris arrived at Tubman High Tuesday morning, he saw Kevin Walker talking to somebody in a Mercedes Benz. Kevin was laughing with the guy. Then Kevin backed off, and the guy drove away. Jaris walked toward Kevin. "Hey, man, that wasn't Cory Yates you were talking to, was it? I thought that dude was in prison for a DUI and drug possession."

"He plea-bargained the drug charges. He's fightin' the DUI. He's got some ambulance-chasing lawyer on his side. Figures he can beat the rap," Kevin explained.

"Man," Jaris fumed, "my little sister and her friends were in Anderson Middle School when he conned them into a car

ride with him." Anger ran like a hot wire
through Jaris's voice. "That dude was goin'
over a hundred miles an hour with kids
in the car. What's goin' down here anyway? And, like, maybe a better question
is, why're you hangin' with scum like him,
Kev? Cory your new bro or what?"

"Hey, Gramma," Kevin sneered, "you
gonna ground me 'cause you don't like
who I talk to?"

"Kevin, I'm serious," Jaris snapped.

"Don't get your shorts in a bind, man,"
Kevin insisted. "Cory's trying to straighten
out. He's not some hard core criminal. He's
barely more than a kid himself. What's
with you, Jaris? You got a cop complex or
something? You gotta keep your eye on everybody to make sure they're stayin' on the
straight and narrow?"

Kevin was almost nose to nose with
Jaris now. "Listen," he snarled, "you
need to go to that Holiness Awakening
Church and help old Pastor Bromley as a
deacon or something. You can help him

round up the sinners and deliver them to hell."

Jaris stalked away. Kevin had been talking about how much he wanted some real money, and that he'd do almost anything to get it. Jaris could sympathize with Kevin wanting to help his grandparents out, but wanting—needing—money that desperately was dangerous. It led to getting mixed up with the wrong crowd. Jaris always thought Cory Yates had drug connections in Los Angeles. He was a two-bit hustler, and he spent way too much time hanging around high schools.

Alonee Lennox and Oliver Randall caught up with Jaris as he stomped toward his first class. "You look deep in thought, Jaris," Alonee remarked. "Everything okay?"

"How's the visit going with Sereeta's dad?" Oliver asked, figuring that's what was on Jaris's mind.

"Not so good," Jaris answered. "The guy only stayed one day. He bailed in the middle of the night. My whole family went over to Sereeta's house yesterday morning, and Pop cooked breakfast. That was nice. It seemed to cheer Sereeta up. Then Pop packed a picnic lunch, and me and Sereeta went up to the beach. Mom and Pop were both awesome."

Jaris's thoughts were now on Sereeta. "I expected Pop to come through," he continued. "But Mom was just as great. She's had her misgivings about Sereeta and me, but yesterday she treated Sereeta like her own daughter. It was beautiful. I could just see the hurt going out of Sereeta's eyes."

"Sereeta here yet?" Alonee asked, looking around.

"Not yet. I'm hanging here at Harriet Tubman's statue waiting for her," Jaris replied as he scanned the parking lot. While still on the lookout for Sereeta, his mind floated back to Kevin and Cory Yates.

"Hey, Oliver, Alonee," he asked, "did you guys see that Mercedes out in front of the school a few minutes ago. Cory Yates was driving it."

"Yeah, not good," Oliver commented.

"We need to tell them in the office," Alonee advised. "Security needs to get after it. Yates loitering around, maybe trying to sell drugs to the freshmen."

"Kevin was talking to Cory," Jaris stated.

"Yeah?" Oliver asked, frowning.

"Kevin's a good guy, but he hangs with bad dudes sometimes," Jaris remarked. "I'm scared he'll get in over his head one of these days."

"Kevin still working at the pizza place?" Oliver asked.

"Yeah," Jaris answered, "but since Eddie Fry bought the place, business has been skidding. He's a miser, and he cuts back on ingredients. The pizzas are awful, and the tips are way down. The guy who used to run the place had those great pineapple pizzas, and business was booming."

Then Jaris saw Sereeta riding up on her bicycle. He excused himself and walked over to her as she was locking up her bike. "Hey, babe!" Jaris greeted, giving her a hug.

"Hi, Jaris," Sereeta said. "You guys were so great yesterday. I love your mom and dad and Chelsea. What a tribe you belong to, Jaris. Do you think it would be too late for them to adopt me?"

"No can do," Jaris laughed. "Then I'd be dating my sister."

Sereeta laughed too. She seemed over the worst of her disappointment with her father's visit. "You entering your story in that contest today, Jaris?" she asked.

"Yeah. The judges are Mr. Myers, Ms. Eloise Jones, the lady who teaches Shakespeare, and a couple of other guys in the English department," Jaris replied.

"And you didn't even let me read it," Sereeta scolded as they walked toward English.

"I'm embarrassed," Jaris explained. "I didn't let anybody read it. Mom was nagging me to read it. I keep thinking it's really awful, and I must be crazy to think I could win a prize."

"What's the title, Jaris?" Sereeta asked.

" 'The Rings of Saturn,' " Jaris said.

"Can't you give me a hint on what it's about?" Sereeta asked. "We just saw the rings of Saturn the other night. Did that give you an idea?"

"Kinda. I just don't want to tell you about it. Then you'll maybe think it's stupid," Jaris responded. "Then I'll see a funny look on your face, but because you're so sweet, you'll say it sounds wonderful."

"Jaris, your insecurities are jumping up and biting you again," Sereeta advised.

"Tell me about it," Jaris said. "I'm better now than I used to be. Poor Pop still fights the same battles. He always used to put himself down as just an old grease monkey, but owning the garage has helped loads. I see him sometimes just looking up at that sign—Spain's Auto Care—and he's smiling. That makes me so happy."

Jaris felt happy for the moment, thinking about his pop and his business. "I have this dream of graduating from Tubman with a good GPA," Jaris went on, "and doing good in college, teaching, maybe writing. If I could even get an honorable mention for my story, it would mean so much to me. I don't expect the story to get one of the money prizes, but there's five honorable mentions and a little certificate comes with them. I'd be thrilled with just one of those."

At lunchtime that day, the group of friends who called themselves "Alonee's posse" gathered under the eucalyptus trees. Jaris was happy to see Trevor Jenkins coming with his new girlfriend, Denique Giles. They were both laughing and being comfortable with everybody.

But Kevin Walker was missing.

"Where's Kevin, Carissa?" Jaris asked Kevin's girlfriend, Carissa Polson.

"I don't know," Carissa replied. "I thought he'd be here. We're growing plums out where I live, and he loves plums. I brought some for him."

Jaris knew it was none of his business, and Kevin would be angry at him for asking Carissa. But Jaris spoke up anyway. "You know about that dude Cory Yates, Carissa?"

"No, who's he?" Carissa asked, opening her sandwich.

"He's some creep who's mixed up with drugs and stuff. I saw him here this morning in his silver Mercedes," Jaris explained.

"Oh!" Carissa exclaimed. "*That* guy. I think he's a friend of Kevin's. But Kevin said he got clean in rehab and now he's selling insurance or something."

"If you believe that, Carissa," Jaris sneered, "then let me tell you about the UFO they're hiding in the science building. Cory Yates and his little brother, Brandon, almost got my sister and her friends killed while they were students at Anderson Middle School. He tricked them into taking this wild ride around town and on the freeway.

Cory got a DUI and was busted on drug possession, but now I guess he's wriggling out of it. I hate to see Kevin hanging with a creep like that."

Carissa laughed sharply. "You don't tell Kevin what to do if you know what's good for you, Jaris." Carissa was a beautiful girl with corn row hair and big, expressive eyes. She and Kevin had their ups and downs, but right now they seemed very close.

"When I try to tell Kevin he's stepping over the line in something," she advised, "he gives me that look, Jaris. He's his own guy. Nobody tells him what to do or what not to do."

"Yeah, Carissa, but he's my friend and I care about him," Jaris insisted. "I don't want him getting mixed up in something that's gonna ruin his life. He's a good-looking, athletic guy, and he's smart. It would be a rotten shame if Yates led him down some road that ended up on the wrong side of the law. Sometimes there's no coming back."

"Maybe his grandparents could get a heads-up on who he's hanging with," Oliver suggested. "Kevin respects them."

"Yeah," Jaris agreed. "That's a good idea, Oliver. After school will you go out to their place with me? I don't have to report to the Chicken Shack till five, so we'd have time to talk to them. I know that Kevin has to work at the pizza place after school today, so he wouldn't be there."

"Yeah, sure I will," Oliver said. "He's my friend too. He did me a favor once that I'll never forget. Marko was being a real stinker, insulting my father, and I lost my cool. I was gonna go after Marko, but Kevin grabbed my arm and stopped me. Who knows what might have happened if he hadn't done that. I owe the guy."

"You know what," Alonee chimed in. "Kevin's grandparents are hard up. They had some little investments that tanked, and now they're struggling. Why don't you guys buy one of those honey-glazed hams and bring them that? You can pretend you got an extra one and you didn't know what to do with it, so you wouldn't hurt their pride." Alonee reached into her purse. "I'll kick in for it."

"Me too," Sereeta added, tossing her bills into the pile. "Get a nice big ham. They're so delicious."

Derrick, Trevor, Destini, Matson Malloy, and Sami Archer added their bills. There was now money enough for the honey-glazed ham, some cheeses, a couple loaves of rye bread, and sparkling apple juice.

"So what's our story, Jaris?" Oliver asked.

"Uh … we won a bunch of food in a raffle and when we took our share, this stuff was left," he said. "It was just going to go to waste, so we thought of taking it out to the Stevens's house."

"Sounds good," Oliver declared. "Just so we're on the same page."

"I'm glad you guys are doing this," Matson said suddenly. "One time when Marko Lane was really ridin' me, I was so

71

depressed I wanted to die. I fumbled the baton in a relay race, and Marko almost tore my head off. Kevin comes along, and he talks to me for maybe an hour. He tells me that this great gold medalist, Wilma Rudolph, fumbled the baton in a relay race too. You don't know what that meant to me. The guy picked me up outta a deep hole."

"Yeah," Jaris agreed, "Kevin has such a good heart. That's why I'm not gonna let him get in trouble. I'm just not."

On this day, English was scheduled right after lunch. As the students filed into class, Langston Myers was standing at his desk. He had a large cardboard tray on his desk bearing the title "Short Story Contest Entries." Jaris had already filled out the entry form. Now he placed the manila envelope containing his story and a disk of it in the tray.

"Ah, you're entering the contest," Mr. Myers noted approvingly. "You have aspirations to be a writer?"

"Well, I'll probably be a teacher, and then maybe I'll write too," Jaris responded. "I don't know."

"Writing is an excellent way for a teacher to spread ideas beyond the limited world of the classroom," Mr. Myers remarked. Since his own novel had been published, even though he had to pay to have it published, Mr. Myers was in a much better mood during his classes. Having a book with his name on the spine made him immensely proud.

Jaris noted about five other manila envelopes in the tray, and he thought they were all probably better than his. Then the class bell rang, and Mr. Myers began his class.

After school, Jaris and Oliver shopped for the food and brought it over to Kevin's grandparents' house. When they arrived, Kevin's grandfather, Roy Stevens, was in the front yard tending a pathetic-looking tomato patch. Mr. Stevens turned slowly on his arthritic legs and hailed the boys.

"Hello there, Jaris, Oliver," he called to them. "What brings ya here?"

Jaris and Oliver got out of the car.

"You know, Mr. Stevens," Oliver said, "this raffle gave away a bunch of food, and we can't use it all. Ya think you could use it?" Oliver opened the trunk as Mr. Stevens stepped over to the car.

Roy Stevens peered in the trunk. "Well now! Looks like mighty fine stuff there. If you're of a mind to, just bring it on in, boys."

Jaris and Oliver carried it all into the house.

"Boys said it was all left over," Roy Stevens explained. "They didn't want it going to waste."

"Lord all mighty!" Lena exclaimed. "A honey-glazed ham! And fancy cheese. This is wonderful. You boys are heaven-sent. Social Security check don't stretch as far as it used to."

Mrs. Stevens served the boys glasses of ice-cold lemonade and started putting the food away.

"So," Jaris asked, slugging his lemonade. "How's everything going here?"

"We can't complain," Roy replied. "We're still able to do what we need to do, and looks like the good Lord is keepin' us here for a purpose. I think it's to raise the boy, to see Kevin till he's a man—see him through."

"We promised our daughter when she was dyin' that we'd see the boy through," Mrs. Stevens explained. "All we ask is that he becomes a good man. That's all we're asking for."

"He's a good boy, but he's strong-willed," Roy commented.

Jaris and Oliver exchanged worried looks. This old couple didn't need to hear that their precious grandson was keeping bad company and that he needed some reigning in. But if they didn't tell them, they'd be denying them a chance to turn Kevin around before it was too late.

"Kevin's a great guy," Jaris opened. "He's one of our best friends. But you know, there are some bad influences around Tubman High. Most of the kids are fine, but we got these creeps lurking on the edge. They try to lure the good kids in with promises of big money."

"Yeah," Oliver chimed in. "Kevin's eager to help you guys out, and sometimes he doesn't think he's doing enough."

Lena Stevens smiled. "The boy's so good. We love him dearly. He's our whole life," she remarked.

"There's one guy in particular that we're worried about," Jaris told the couple. "His name's Cory Yates, and he's been trying to get close to Kevin. I think he's telling Kevin that if you cut a few corners, you can make easy money. Y'hear what I'm saying?"

The old couple looked alarmed.

"Kevin hanging out with this Cory Yates? Is that what you're saying, Jaris?" Roy Stevens asked.

"He's talking to him, that's all," Jaris replied. "I just thought maybe you guys might tell him to be careful. Bad dudes like Yates could hurt him, y'know? Maybe coming from you, he'd listen."

"Jaris tried to talk to Kevin, but he didn't take it too well. But he respects you folks," Oliver added.

Roy and Lena Stevens looked at each other with fear in their eyes.

"Oh, my precious Lord!" Lena gasped, hardly above a whisper. "It's like what happened with his daddy, with Kevin's daddy. He was a good boy, but he fell in with bad sorts, and they pulled him down and down."

Roy Stevens looked at Jaris and Oliver. "You know about Kevin's daddy, don't you?" he asked sorrowfully.

"Yeah," Jaris replied, "we know."

Kevin's father had fought another man and killed him. He ended up in prison for murder, and he died there in a prison riot. Kevin knew he had his father's temper, and he fought to control it. But now he needed to fight against something else: wanting money so badly that he'd do anything to get it, even something Cory Yates might suggest.

"Thank you for caring enough about Kevin that you'd come out to talk to us," Roy Stevens told the boys. "And thank you for all the wonderful food."

"Kevin's lucky to have friends like you boys," Lena added. "You're a blessing. And we *will* talk to the boy."

CHAPTER FIVE

On Wednesday, Jaris was at the vending machine wondering whether any navel oranges were available. He was looking into the little compartments when he heard a sharp voice behind him.

"Hey, thanks a lot, man, for going out to my house and telling my grandparents I was throwing in with dopehead gangbangers," Kevin snapped.

"I didn't say that, Kevin," Jaris responded, trying to keep his cool. "I just told them you were getting too friendly with Cory Yates. He's a bad guy, Kevin, and you don't see anything wrong with hanging with him. I talked to your grandparents 'cause they have a right to know.

We're seventeen, dude. We don't know it all yet."

"Except for you," Kevin sneered bitterly. "You know it all. You don't have a problem with stickin' your nose into other people's business. Well, lissen up, man. You're not my father. You're not my grandfather. Stop messin' with my life and scarin' those old people out there over nothing. You shoulda seen them. Grandma was all shaky and near tears. That's *your* fault, man."

"No," Jaris insisted. "It's *your* fault, Kevin. You know what they went through when your dad stepped over the line and died young. You know what stepping over the line did to your father. You're their life, man. You gotta walk the line."

"I'm walking the line, dude," Kevin snarled, "but it's gonna be *my* line, not *yours*." With that, he turned and stomped away.

Trevor Jenkins had been at the edge of the conversation and had heard much of it. "Hoo-boy!" he exclaimed. "There's a tickin' time bomb if I've ever seen one, Jaris."

"Yeah, I know," Jaris sighed. "And what bothers me most of all is that he's such a good guy. If he was a creep, I wouldn't bother with him."

"Can't Carissa get through to him?" Trevor asked.

"I already asked her. She's afraid of getting on his bad side. She's walking on eggshells with him," Jaris explained.

"Man," Trevor remarked, "Denique doesn't have that problem with me. She speaks her mind, man. I'm doing something she doesn't like, and she yells at me. She's like Ma!"

Jaris smiled. "That's you, Trevor. And Denique, I gotta hand it to that chick. She's not afraid of anything. But Carissa's different. Carissa tells Kevin what she thinks he wants to hear. She stepped over the line once and saw another guy, and she almost lost him for good. Now she's doubly careful. She doesn't want to risk losing him again."

"If he throws in with Cory Yates, we *all* lose him," Trevor noted.

"You got that right, man," Jaris agreed sadly.

Jaris didn't know what Cory was into now, but he figured it had to be something illegal. If it wasn't drugs, it was a scam of some kind. Whatever it was, Jaris hoped Kevin wouldn't get mixed up in it.

At dinner that night, Chelsea told her parents something that had happened at lunch. "Maurice had a joint, and Inessa made him get rid of it," Chelsea announced.

"That lousy little punk," Pop snarled. "I knew he was no good when he was hanging around out there in the street acting like a big shot. Where did he get it, little girl?"

"Some creepy guy sold it to him," Chelsea answered. "I told Jaris, and he said it was Cory Yates."

"Yeah," Jaris chimed in. "Alonee Lennox went to Mr. Hawthorne and told him today. Hawthorne's kinda wimpy. He doesn't take care of business, but I think he'll do something about this. He said he'd tell the school security and call the cops too. I don't think Cory Yates is gonna be hanging around Tubman anymore. Mr. Hawthorne doesn't really pay attention around school. He shoulda seen the Mercedes parked there in the morning himself."

"He's a sniveling little bureaucrat like most of those so-called educators," Pop snorted.

"Lorenzo," Mom chided, "most teachers and administrators are doing their level best to protect the kids from the drug dealers and all the other stuff going on. It was much easier in the old days. The big problem used to be kids chewing gum in class. Now it's not uncommon to have several kids high in middle school. We even had a little girl in my school the other day high on her mom's cold medicine."

"Don't have nothin' to do with that Maurice, little girl," Pop commanded his daughter.

"Heston told me he never smoked anything," Chelsea remarked. "Not even regular cigarettes 'cause they hurt your lungs. The other kids asked me if I ever tried weed. For a minute, I was afraid to sound like a Goody Two-shoes, but then I said I never did. Heston said he was real proud of me for that."

"Yeah, that Heston, he's all right," Pop commented.

"He really likes me. He's kinda shy so he doesn't say much, but I can tell he really likes me," Chelsea confided.

"Just so he don't like you too much, little girl," Pop noted, "if y'hear what I'm sayin'."

The next day, Thursday, on their way to class, Jaris asked Sereeta if she had told her mother about her father coming down to visit.

"Yeah," Sereeta replied. "We talked about it yesterday. Jare, I had such a strange day yesterday. It was weird, but in some way wonderful. I picked up Mom after school in Grandma's Volvo, and then we got Jake at day care. We went to the park where the new play equipment is in. We put Jake down with his toys, and Mom and I sat there on a bench, talking. A little old lady came along, and she looks at us. She thinks I'm Jake's mother and Mom is the grandma. She beams at us and says to Mom, 'What a beautiful young grandma you are. I bet you're a proud grandma too.' "

Sereeta chuckled and went on. "I kinda winced 'cause you know how Mom fears growing older. I thought that would send her into a fit of depression, but she just laughed. You know what she said? She told the lady that Jake was her younger baby and I was her older baby. It was kind of cute. Oh, Jaris, Mom *is* getting better. *She really is*."

"Yeah, that is a good sign," Jaris agreed, overjoyed at Sereeta's happiness.

"Then I told her about Dad talking all the time about the stepsons and how he sneaked out a day early in the dead of night," Sereeta continued. "I told Mom how you guys showed up in the morning like the cavalry and saved the day. You guys turned what would have been a bad, weepy day into a good day. Mom laughed. She was so glad about what you guys did."

Jaris looked over at his girl and saw that she was smiling. "I thought maybe Mom would say some ugly things about how Dad acted," Sereeta said, "but she didn't. She even said my father tried when they were married. He tried, but it just wasn't meant to be."

Sereeta took Jaris's hand and gave it a shake while they walked. "And you know what the best part of the whole day was?" she asked. "I never thought you'd hear me say this, but I'm falling in love with Jake. He's so cute and sweet. Mom talked to her doctor about how she was feeling about the baby, and she said she's not to feel bad. She told Mom that lots of moms go through it and they can be helped. They end up loving their babies just fine."

"That's all great, Sereeta," Jaris responded.

"Yeah," Sereeta said. "I guess the secret is if you just hang in there long enough, things turn around and get better."

She paused then and commented, "Kevin's mad at you, isn't he?"

"What makes you say that, Sereeta?" Jaris asked.

"I asked him why he's not coming around to eat lunch with us," Sereeta explained. "He made some nasty comment about you sticking your nose into his business, and he's tired of it."

"He'll be okay," Jaris replied without much conviction.

That night, Jaris didn't have to work at the Chicken Shack, so he did his homework and went to bed early for him—ten thirty. He wanted to get a good night's sleep so that he'd be up for a great weekend with Sereeta. He thought maybe they'd go to one of those amusement parks. He'd pick a really wild roller coaster, so he could hold Sereeta in his arms while she screamed.

Just before he went to sleep, Jaris was thinking about Kevin. He felt sad that they weren't friends right now. Jaris hoped things would all blow over soon. Jaris missed Kevin at lunchtime. Kevin added spice to the camaraderie.

"Jaris!" Chelsea yelled from the hallway, pushing Jaris's bedroom door open. "It was just on the news! They robbed the pizza place!"

"Where Kevin works?" Jaris gasped, sitting up in bed. His first thought was that Kevin might've gotten hurt.

"Yeah," Chelsea reported, "Ace's Pizza."

"Did they say if anybody was hurt?" Jaris asked, trying to remember if this was one of Kevin's nights on the job. Jaris felt weak in the knees as he rolled out of bed and slipped on a robe. Chelsea scurried back to the living room.

"No, no one hurt," Chelsea answered. "They said the owner was taking the cash to a night deposit box, and somebody got him in the parking lot. Jaris, the guy had a gun, and he took all the money and left the owner bound and gagged with duct tape. Some guy walking his dog found him lying there helpless."

"Oh man, that's awful!" Jaris moaned. Jaris called the Stevens's house. He hated to bother them at ten forty-five, but he was worried about Kevin. Lena Stevens answered.

"Hi, this is Jaris Spain. I tried Kevin on his cell, and I was transferred to voice mail," Jaris explained. "I hate to bother you guys. Did Kevin work tonight?"

"No, he didn't," Lena Stevens answered. "He should be home anytime now. I think he went to a boxing match with that boy Lydell. They do that a lot. Should I give him a message for you, Jaris?"

"No, thank you, Mrs. Stevens," Jaris responded. "I'll catch him tomorrow." Jaris decided not to say anything about the robbery. Let Kevin tell them. Jaris didn't want to get into anymore trouble with Kevin Walker.

Jaris went into the living room, where Mom and Pop were watching the news. "How awful!" Mom commented. "An armed robbery right down the street from here."

"Any description of the robber?" Jaris asked.

"Stocking cap and ski mask kind of guy," Pop grumbled, grimacing.

"I'm glad Kevin wasn't working there tonight," Jaris noted. "Sometimes he makes the night deposit."

Kevin had told Jaris a lot about his boss, Eddie Fry, who was in his fifties. He'd taken over a thriving pizza shop and run it into the ground by offering a poor product.

The dumpsters behind the place were over-flowing with half-eaten pizzas. Eddie Fry's son, Jex, worked there too, but Kevin said he was a lazy guy and not much help.

"Somebody hadda get to know the man's routine," Pop guessed. "Big mistake to make it a habit to go a certain route every night with the deposit. At the garage, not too many people pay in cash, but I take the money in at different times. Never at night. I'm always watchin' too. Nobody gonna sneak up on Lorenzo Spain."

Jaris stood there staring at the television screen. The robber had probably been cas-ing the joint for a while, he thought. Ace's Pizza had a special deal on Thursday: regu-lar price for a big pizza and the second one for half price. Although business was never as good anymore, Thursday was the best night. The robber must have known this would be the best time for a score.

A horrible thought crossed Jaris's mind, like a snake coiled to strike. Could Kevin be somehow involved? Could he have tipped off Cory Yates that old Fry always crossed the dark parking lot with his night deposit on Thursday night?

Jaris dismissed the thought right away, but there it was for a few seconds. Kevin would never be mixed up in an armed robbery, where somebody could get hurt or killed. Maybe, if his back was to the wall, he'd get involved in some scam, but never in something with guns. It wasn't in him.

Jaris tried Kevin's cell phone many more times, but he was always turned over to voice mail. He left no message.

Jaris didn't get the good night's sleep he was hoping for.

CHAPTER SIX

On Friday, Jaris approached Harriet Tubman's statue at the entrance to the school. There he saw Kevin, Lydell Nelson, and Derrick Shaw talking. When Jaris walked up, Kevin asked, "You heard, huh?"

"Yeah, tough," Jaris replied.

"It's so stupid," Kevin snapped. "I told Fry to stop doin' that. He didn't need to get that night deposit in. Coulda stayed in the store safe until morning. But the old fool wouldn't listen. He never listens to anybody. That's how he's ruined the business. He's so freaked out by the robbery that he's shutting down the shop for a few days."

Kevin shook his head in disgust. "Fry, he said he almost got a heart attack when that robber came up behind him. He said when he saw the gun, he freaked. Now me and the other guys got no paycheck. I was supposed to work tonight and Saturday. That's when the best tips come in. It's really gonna hurt. What a stupid bummer."

"I know what you're sayin', dude," Derrick said. "I count on every dollar I make where I work. Waleed, my boss, he's smart. He has somebody else come in for the cash, different cousins and like that. Nobody knows what's goin' on. You gotta be careful."

Lydell Nelson chimed in. "I'm glad I got this little teacher's aide job with Mr. Myers. It doesn't pay much, but it helps. I get my spending money. I don't have to beg for a few dollars at home where they don't like me anyway." Lydell had no parents, and he lived with reluctant family members. They begrudged him everything.

"They said on TV that the robber wore a stocking cap and a ski mask," Jaris remarked.

"Yeah," Kevin said. "I talked to the other guy who works there, and he said Fry can't give a decent description of the thug. He was too scared. Can't say how tall, how heavy, nothin'."

A shadow crossed Kevin's face then as he looked at Jaris. "Hey, dude, when I got home from the fights last night, my grandparents said you called the house. What for?"

"I heard about the robbery at the place where you worked, man," Jaris explained. "I thought you mighta been hurt or something."

Kevin didn't say anything. He gave Jaris a strange look before turning and walking away with Lydell.

"Uh-oh," Jaris thought. "He figures I think he was maybe involved in the robbery. That's why I called his grandparents. I was checking to see if he was home. That's why he gave me that dirty look."

At lunchtime, all the regulars showed up under the eucalyptus trees, including

Kevin and Carissa. Lydell Nelson came too, which was unusual.

"Lotta students submitting stories for the contest, Jaris," Lydell advised. "Mr. Myers is really excited. He's been taking them home and reading them. I'd sure like to win one of the top three, but I don't think so."

"Yeah, I don't think my story'll bubble to the top either," Jaris replied.

"You know," Lydell said, "I like being a teaching assistant for Mr. Myers. I know he's got a big ego, but he's a cool guy."

"I enjoy him in class," Jaris noted.

Kevin lay back on the grass, resting his head in Carissa's lap, as he often did. He looked troubled. Jaris thought he was worried about his job at Ace's Pizza. He needed the money he made. Now it was all up in the air.

Pop came home from the shop Friday night just before Jaris left for work at the Chicken Shack. Pop was furious. "You guys'll never guess who I saw strollin' down the street today?" Pop announced.

"Who?" Mom asked.

"None other than the little creep that I caught trying to steal from my cash drawer," Pop answered. "Monie, 'member when I first started the garage under my own name? This kid, Boston Blake, pulled a knife on me when I collared him. He's out on bail, you guys, free as a bird. His folks came through with the bail, and he gets to walk until his trial comes up. Then he'll probably plea-bargain to disorderly conduct or something."

"Oh, my goodness!" Mom sighed. "That's terrible. He's a dangerous person. He threatened you with a knife, Lorenzo. He should never have gotten bail."

"Oh no, babe!" Pop shouted. "He's just a poor, misunderstood little punk. That's the story they're sellin'. He's the salt o' the earth. He never meant no harm. Just wanted to borrow a few bills from the cash drawer. When I come in there and stopped him, he was scared. He thought I was gonna kill him. He pulled the knife in self-defense, yeah. That mean ol' grease monkey had no business stoppin' this fine, upstandin' young dude from stealin'."

Pop stood in the living room, his head nodding back and forth in frustration. "I'm tellin' ya, Monie," he ranted, "our justice system is all screwed up. We might as well not have a system. I'm tellin' you, I'm about ready to go back to the way they done it in the Old West. You steal a horse at noon, you're dancing in the air at sundown."

Jaris shook his head sadly. "If he comes near the garage, Pop, call nine-one-one. He might have something bad on his mind."

"Oh, I ain't scared of that little dirtbag," Pop declared. "Our eyes met today, and he looked scared. He knows that if he showed up at the garage, I'd turn 'im upside down and use 'im like a mop."

Jaris drove to the Chicken Shack, glad at least that the problem with Amberlynn

Parson was solved. She had a crush on him, and the Tubman students were gossiping that Jaris liked her too. Jaris had finally made things clear to Amberlynn. He wasn't going to risk Sereeta being hurt by the groundless gossip that something was going on with Amberlynn and Jaris.

"Hey, Trevor," Jaris said when he arrived at the Chicken Shack. "Neal better be careful making deposits. We got a robber in the neighborhood hitting fast-food places."

Neal came around the corner. "You guys know the drill, right? If a guy with a gun shows up, I don't want you getting hurt. Give him whatever's in the cash drawer. No heroics. I make sure we don't have too much in the cash drawers. The rest is in the safe, and nobody around here has the combination to the safe. Only the big boss does. See the posted signs? 'No more than one hundred dollars in cash on hand. Employees do not have access to the safe.' That's a real safety plus for us."

"Oh, I'd die of fright if somebody showed up with a gun," Amberlynn remarked.

"Probably won't happen. Whoever hit the pizza place is probably up in LA by now," Neal assured her.

"I know one merchant in town who keeps a gun. He says he'll take out anybody who comes to rob him," Trevor commented.

"That's stupid," Neal snapped. "That's how you get yourself or your people killed. Money is just dirty paper, not worth dying for."

Early in the evening, Marko Lane and his girlfriend, Jasmine Benson, came in. Marko immediately started to tell Amberlynn how he wrestled the gun away from a dangerous psycho and saved the lives of a woman, two children, and Sereeta Prince.

"Weren't you scared?" Amberlynn asked.

"No, I'm pretty cool in situations like that," Marko asserted, grinning. Jasmine rolled her eyes. She had heard this story so many times that she was ready to strangle Marko if he told it one more time.

"Believe me, girl," Marko boasted, "if it'd been me at Ace's Pizza, I woulda ripped that dude's ski mask off and beat him to a pulp. He wouldna got no money from me. No way. I'd of taken that gun away from him just like I did with that psycho. Nobody messes with Marko Lane."

Marko glanced over at Jaris, who had just finished taking an order. "Jaris, you were there," Marko said to him. "You saw me in action. Ain't I telling the honest truth? Didn't it come down just like I'm tellin' it, man? You saw the whole thing. Didn't I march up to that bad guy and take his gun right away from him? Didn't I save that poor woman and her kids and Sereeta too?"

"Yep," Jaris admitted. "It really did happen that way."

"You see, Amberlynn," Marko said. "You're looking at a hero right here, girl. That old man holding the hostages, he was crazy and drunk. He mighta killed everybody before he got done there. But he didn't count on having to deal with Marko Lane."

"Marko," Jasmine moaned, "you *ever* gonna quit bragging on that?"

Marko looked offended. "Girl, you oughta be proud of your man. Not every chick gets to hang out with a hero," he told her. "You oughta be bustin' with pride."

"Maybe you should get one of these suits like Superman or Spiderman wears," Trevor remarked. "You could be Markoman."

"You're makin' light of it, dude," Marko sneered. "On account of you not bein' a hero. I'm not tryin' to put you down, man, but you're not the hero type. You're scared of your own shadow, Trevor." Marko looked around, laughing, "This boy here is scared of his own mama."

Trevor shrugged and admitted it. "That's true I guess, but only somebody who never seen my mama would laugh at that."

It was a busy Friday night with a lot of customers coming in. Once, a young man came in alone, looking nervous. When Jaris saw him—someone he didn't know—his guard went up. He breathed a sigh of relief when the guy left.

Close to quitting time, the crowd thinned out. The only ones in the Chicken Shack were Jaris, Neal, Trevor, Amberlynn, and an old man in one of the booths, lingering over his coffee. Then a sullen-looking young man walked in, and the chills went up Jaris's spine again.

Jaris's imagination started working overtime. What if the dude pulled a gun? They'd give him what they had, but what if that wasn't enough? What if he started shooting up the place out of pure spite? In an incident in Texas, a guy killed three hamburger joint employees even though they had cooperated with him.

Amberlynn noticed the young man too. She looked tense. "Amberlynn," Jaris ordered, "go back in the kitchen and ask Neal if we got enough packets of mayo for tomorrow."

"There's plenty—" she started to say, then she understood. She turned and hurried back into the kitchen. As she disappeared around the corner, Jaris saw near terror on her face.

Jaris looked at the young man, now approaching the counter. "What'll it be?" he asked.

"Chicken sandwich and side salad," the man replied.

"Ranch or vinaigrette on the salad?" Jaris asked, his voice a little shaky. He was overreacting, he knew, but the guy didn't look right.

"Ranch," the customer answered, reaching into his pocket.

Jaris thought silently, "Make him be reaching for his wallet, not a gun. Please make him be reaching for his wallet."

"Grilled or crispy on the sandwich?" Jaris asked.

"Grilled," the guy said, pulling out a wrinkled five dollar bill and putting it on the counter.

"Four fifty out of five," Jaris said, putting the change in the man's hand. "For here or to go?"

"To go," he responded.

Within minutes, the man was out the door with his bag.

Jaris leaned on the counter. He exchanged looks with Trevor. They needed no words. The relief was in their eyes, in the way their shoulders slumped. Amberlynn came slowly back to the front. "Is he gone?" she asked.

"He's gone," Jaris replied. "All he wanted was a chicken sandwich and a side salad after all."

Amberlynn laughed nervously. "I thought—"

"Yeah, me too," Trevor said.

"Likewise," Jaris added.

"You sent me to the back because you thought there was gonna be trouble," Amberlynn noted.

"I thought we might be low on the mayo packages," Jaris lied. He didn't want to start anything. He didn't want her thinking he was looking out for her in a special way. But the truth was that she was a chick.

What he thought of her wouldn't have mattered. She was a chick. You try to protect them if you're any kind of man. It'd bad enough to have a guy at the counter if something bad went down. But you didn't want a chick there.

"We're sitting ducks in these places," Trevor commented. "Places that are open all night. The creeps are roaming around looking for places that stay open late or all night. It's even worse at the twenty-four-seven stores. But we're all sitting ducks when the lights come on and the moon goes up."

"Yeah," Jaris agreed.

"My ma says when your time comes, it comes," Trevor stated. "I'm not sure if I think that way or not. She says if you're on the battlefield over there where my brother Desmond is, or if you're in your own bed, it don't matter. When your time is up, it's up. Ma is a great believer in the will of the Lord. That's why she never misses singing in the praise chorus at the Holiness Awakening Church every Sunday."

"Well, I guess it's a good way to think," Jaris responded. "Kinda takes the pressure off worrying about every little thing. But I'm real glad tonight wasn't my time."

Jaris laughed shakily. He knew he let his imagination get the best of him. The sullen-looking guy was just hungry, but who knew? Something bad could happen so fast. One minute you're planning your weekend at the amusement park, and the next minute someone else is planning your funeral.

But it didn't happen. Jaris heaved a sigh of relief and started getting the store ready to be shut down. As he did, he thought about his story in the contest. He thought about being with Sereeta tomorrow, having fun at the amusement park, being on the rides, and eating unhealthy food.

Before Jaris went home, Neal talked to him. "Jenny told me she's gonna have another baby," he announced, "and she needs to be home with the kids, Jaris. She's ready to quit right now, but she's willing to stay on until we can hire a good replacement.

She's getting that morning sickness stuff, so the sooner the better, Jaris. You bein' the assistant manager, you do the hiring, Jaris. You did such a great job hiring Amberlynn. The customers all love her, and she's really efficient. So I'm giving you the heads-up, Jaris."

"Okay, Neal, I'll get the word out. I'll hire somebody as soon as I find a good one," Jaris promised. "One more thing, though. Amberlynn is ready for a raise. She's met all the requirements for a new employee. In fact, she'd done way better. Can you fix that, Neal?"

"Sure, figured that," Neal responded. "There'll be a nice increase in her check next time, Jaris. She's been great for business. She has it coming."

"Thanks, man," Jaris said.

When the store was closed, Jaris headed for the parking lot. He noticed Mr. Parson pulling up outside in his pickup truck. Amberlynn was hurrying to get in. Jaris sprinted over before the truck got away.

"Evening, Mr. Parson. Amberlynn, Neal was just telling me what a great worker you are. There'll be more money in your paycheck next week."

"Oh!" Amberlynn responded with a big smile. "Thanks, Jaris."

"No thanks to me," Jaris objected. "You earned it. Goodnight now."

On his drive home, Jaris recognized several familiar cars at the Ice House. Marko Lane and Jasmine were there. No doubt Marko had found more people to listen to his story. Kevin Walker's beat-up ex-stock car was there too.

Jaris checked the time. He had a few extra minutes, so he pulled into the parking lot at the Ice House. As he did, Kevin and Carissa were walking out. Jaris stopped the car and opened his door. "Hey, Kevin, Carissa," he called out.

Kevin had a terrible look on his face. Carissa looked extremely upset. Jaris felt sorry for her. Something bad had to have happened.

"He's blaming me, dude," Kevin fumed.

"Who is? What're you sayin', man?" Jaris asked.

"Old man Fry," Kevin snarled. "He's saying I musta set him up for one of my sleazy friends when he got mugged. He's saying the guy was lying in wait for him. The guy had to know. Fry, he found out about my father. He said he never woulda hired me in if he knew my father was a killer. He said I lied on the application 'cause I didn't put that in. But it asked if I'd ever been arrested. It never asked about my father."

Kevin sounded more depressed than Jaris had ever seen him. "Old Fry, he goes 'like father, like son,' and then he cans me. The old devil is saying I had something to do with the robbery. He's got no evidence, but he's convicting me 'cause o' my father. How d'ya like that?"

Jaris looked at Kevin. "I'm sorry, man. I really am. But you'll get something else," Jaris assured him. "You'll get a better job.

That pizza place was going down the tubes anyway."

"Everybody knows everybody else around here," Kevin insisted. "Old Fry's spreading the word, and I'll never get another job. I'm guilty without a trial. And let's face it, Jaris, you think I'm a pretty good suspect yourself. Otherwise you wouldna checked me out with my grandparents. *You* don't even trust me, man."

"Kevin, I called your grandparents 'cause I wanted to know if you were working that night. You weren't answering your phone," Jaris insisted. "Look, if you heard the Chicken Shack got robbed, wouldn't you want to know if I was there when it went down. Wouldn't you want to know what happened to me?"

"I gotta go," Kevin snapped, heading for his car. Carissa ran to keep up with him.

CHAPTER SEVEN

When Jaris got home, his parents were still up.

"You guys," he said, "Eddie Fry fired Kevin from the pizza place. Fry's blaming Kevin for the robbery. He thinks some of Kevin's friends did it, and Kevin tipped them off on the timing."

"What a creep!" Pop stormed. "Kevin's a good kid. He wouldn't have nothin' to do with a thing like that."

"I got a decision to make," Jaris said. "You know how Pastor Bromley is always saying one door closes and another one opens up? I just heard tonight that Jenny down at the Chicken Shack wants to quit 'cause she's having another baby. Neal told me to get somebody to take her place. I'm wondering … what do you guys think if I offer the job to Kevin? I've seen him at Ace's Pizza, and he's good. And he'll get better pay than he got at the pizza place."

"I think that's a great idea, Jaris," Pop responded.

Mom looked more skeptical. "Jaris, you've been saying that Kevin has been acting a little strange lately," she noted. "You said he told you he wants money really bad, and he doesn't care what it takes to get it. And you were worried that he was hanging with Cory Yates."

"Yeah, that's true," Jaris admitted. "And he put me on his bad list for sticking my nose into his business. But he's my friend, and he needs a hand up bad."

"Boy," Pop declared, "go with your heart. You ain't gonna go wrong if you go with your heart."

"Lorenzo," Mom objected, "that's not always good advice."

Then she spoke to Jaris. "What if Kevin steals from the till at the Chicken Shack? What if he turns it into a hangout for unsavory characters? Do you know how that's going to make you look, Jaris? You're solely responsible for bringing him in. If it turns out bad, it's on you."

"He wouldn't do stuff like that, Mom," Jaris insisted, but there was a little knot of worry in the pit of his stomach.

"Honey," Mom advised, "you can help Kevin find another job, but I wouldn't bring him into the Chicken Shack. You've only been assistant manager for a short while, and right now Neal thinks you're doing a great job. It could all go up in smoke if you hired a friend and he was bad news."

Jaris sighed deeply and responded to his mother. "Mom, he's going down for the count. He's drowning, and he needs a lifeline now. Eddie Fry's holding it against him that his father was in prison. Fry's spreading poison. Kevin probably can't get another job with that going on."

"Your mom, she thinks with her head and that's good," Pop chimed in. "But sometimes you gotta think with your heart, boy. What'd happen if everybody did what was safe and smart? What if nobody went out on a limb and lent a hand to somebody else without no guarantees? Man, this old world would be an even more miserable place to live in than it already is."

On Saturday morning, Jaris knew that he had to make a decision and that he needed some help with it. He called Trevor.

"Hey, Trev," Jaris said. "I need to talk to you, man."

"Wassup, bro?" Trevor asked. He was Jaris's closest friend. They couldn't have been closer if they had been brothers. Jaris had a lot of faith in Trevor's judgment.

"Trevor, Kevin got canned at the pizza place," Jaris told him. "The dude there is blaming him for the robbery 'cause Kevin has been hanging with some creeps lately. He's saying Kevin set up the hit."

"That's a lotta bull," Trevor snapped hotly.

"Yeah," Jaris agreed. "Right now, Kevin needs a job bad. Jenny's quitting. I'm the assistant manger, and I could get him in there, Trev. What do you think?"

Trevor sounded thoughtful as he spoke. "I'm just wondering if he could handle the counter at the Chicken Shack. Kev's got a bad temper. Some of those customers are a handful. There's a lot more rushing around, lotta pressure, more than he had at that pizza place. I went in that pizza place last week, and there was hardly anybody in there. You know how Kevin explodes, man. If some jerk complained about the cold coffee or something, he might tell him where he could go."

"I hear what you're saying, Trevor," Jaris responded. "But I would make it clear to Kevin that he's got to control his temper." Jaris wasn't sure he could get Kevin to do that. Kevin didn't like to be told anything.

"I don't know, dude," Trevor said. "It sure would be good if you could help the guy out. He needs a job bad. The grandparents need the money he's kicking in. But you'd be laying yourself on the line, man."

Jaris thanked his friend and ended the call.

A little later, when he picked up Sereeta, Jaris told her the problem.

"You know, Sereeta," he told her, "I've known most of you guys all my life. I know just what to expect from all of you. But I've only known Kevin since last year. I like the guy. I really do like him. But do you think I'd be taking a terrible chance to hire him at the Chicken Shack?"

Sereeta laid her small, soft hand on Jaris's hand. "Babe, you want to help him. Everything is a risk, you know. Sometimes we throw our hearts to the wind and hope they don't get broken. Do it. Give him a break, Jaris."

Jaris kissed Sereeta and smiled. They had a wonderful weekend: Saturday on the roller coaster, then Sunday at the beach.

Now it was Monday. Jaris had to make up his mind. Jaris really appreciated his job at the Chicken Shack. Now that he was assistant manager he was doing much better, saving money for college and paying for his Ford Focus. He didn't want to upset his applecart, and yet …

He talked with Derrick Shaw, the first friend he saw on campus. Derrick shook his head. "Dude, I like Kevin, but he's a loose cannon."

Destini, Derrick's girlfriend, agreed. "Don't do it, Jaris. You got too much to lose."

Sami Archer was away on a science field trip, so Jaris couldn't ask her. He wished he could have. She was one of the most compassionate, yet sensible friends he had.

Jaris saw Alonee Lennox and Oliver Randall at the vending machine. He hurried over and told them his problem.

"You guys, old man Fry is blaming the robbery on Kevin and he fired him," Jaris told them. "Kevin really needs another job. I could hire him at the Chicken Shack. Waddya think?"

"Oh, wow, Jaris!" Alonee exclaimed. "Kevin's been acting really weird lately. I went to the pizza place the other night when he was at the counter. He was arguing with some guy about the pizza being cold. Poor Kevin. He was on the verge of throwing the pizza at the guy."

"Did he throw it?" Jaris asked.

"No, but he made me nervous just with his body language," Alonee replied.

"I don't want to risk my own job, you guys," Jaris said, "but Kevin needs help bad. Mom told me I shouldn't risk it, but Pop, he's really got a big heart. He said go for it. Pop yells and rants a lot, but deep down he's really a kindhearted person. He's sort of a marshmallow at heart."

Alonee smiled. "Your pop is a sweetheart, Jaris, but I think your mom's right

119

on this one. I'd hate for you to ruin your own good record at the Chicken Shack after being there so long. I don't know, Jaris. I know what you want to do, but I'm not sure this is right for you."

Jaris looked at Oliver. "Is that pretty much how you feel too, Oliver?" he asked. All the time Alonee was talking, Oliver just listened. Of all Jaris's friends, Oliver Randall was, in Jaris's opinion, the smartest.

Oliver shook his head. "No, Jaris. I think Kevin is treading water right now, and he could drown. I think you have a chance to save him. If you don't try, you'll probably regret it for the rest of your life. Don't refuse the guy a hand, Jaris."

Oliver could tell Jaris was torn. "I'd give you that advice even if I knew Kevin was gonna turn out bad for the job," Oliver added. "At least you will have tried. Compassion is never a mistake, man. I'd rather die because I showed too much compassion than live into old age without pity."

Alonee looked at Jaris and said, "Oliver is big on mercy. He once really went out on a limb for a kid that everybody thought was guilty of a lot of crimes. Oliver was the only one who believed in the kid, and he turned out to be right. I have to admit I wasn't on his side."

"Yeah," Oliver added. "And, Jaris, let me tell you about what happened to my father many years ago, when he was a kid. He was running from the police at night, and one cop snared him. This white cop looked at this black kid, and he thought he had a gun. The cop almost shot the kid— my dad—but he didn't. That cop risked his own life—risked being shot by what looked like a kid with a gun. Except for that act of mercy, my father might have died that night. Dude, you gotta do what's right for you, but I say help Kevin. Give him a break."

Jaris reached out and grabbed Oliver's hand. "Thanks, man," he said softly. Then he hugged Oliver. "Thanks," he repeated.

All morning long, Jaris looked for Kevin, but he was nowhere to be found. At lunchtime, as the gang made its way down the trail to the spot under the eucalyptus trees, Kevin didn't show. Jaris found out he had been in his classes that morning. Right after the last class, Jaris spotted Carissa and called out, "Carissa, is Kevin okay?"

Carissa looked as though she'd been crying. "No," she sighed. "He's crushed and angry. I've never seen him like this. That rotten guy at the pizza place not only fired him, but he said he's gonna try to prove that Kevin was behind the robbery. Jaris, Kevin wouldn't ever do anything like that. It's so unfair. I tried to tell Kevin things would turn out okay, but he just blew me off."

"Did he ditch his classes after lunch?" Jaris asked.

"Yeah, but he said he'd practice with the track team and Coach Curry," Carissa answered. "He said Coach Curry is the only friend he has left. He doesn't want to let him down for the meet that's coming up."

"He's probably over there running right now," Jaris thought out loud.

"I think so, Jaris," Carissa said.

"I need to talk to him, Carissa," Jaris told her.

"I don't think he'll talk to you, Jaris," she advised. "He's mad at everybody. He's mad at you for checking with his grandparents after the robbery. He thinks you believe he was mixed up in that too. Kevin thinks everybody is stabbing him in the back, and he's got nowhere to turn."

"I only wanted to make sure he was okay when I heard about the robbery," Jaris insisted. "Everything I've done, I had only his best interests at heart, Carissa."

"He thinks everybody is against him," Carissa repeated, "including you. He's, like, sunk in a black hole. If I were you, Jaris, I wouldn't even go near him when he's like this. He might hit you. He said some awful things about you."

"I'm pretty good at ducking," Jaris joked. He headed for the athletic field.

"Watch yourself, Jaris" Clarissa called after him.

"Gotta talk to him," Jaris called back. Jaris hoped that maybe doing a few laps had cooled Kevin's temper down a bit.

Jaris stood at the edge of the track and watched Kevin warming up. When Kevin saw him, anger flashed in his face. He stopped his warm ups and stood nose to nose with Jaris.

"What do *you* want?" Kevin demanded. "You want to know where I was when that old devil was getting robbed? You helping build the case against me, man? Well, Officer Spain, you know where you can go."

Jaris's heart was pounding. He'd seen Kevin angry before, but he was over-the-top this time. Everybody, including Kevin himself, knew he had a dangerous temper. He was like his father in that way, subject to rages. But Kevin always fought to keep his anger under control.

But now Kevin Walker's life was falling apart. He didn't see any reason to rein in his temper. He'd lost his job. Nobody else would hire him because of the stories old Fry was spreading. He was under suspicion for an armed robbery. His eyes were filled with fury, even hatred.

Jaris had never been afraid of Kevin before, but now he was. He felt as though he was face to face with an enraged animal.

"Dude," Jaris started to say, forcing his voice to be calm, "I'm not your enemy. I'm your friend if you want to believe it or not. Listen to—"

"Nothing you say I want to hear," Kevin snarled.

Jaris blurted out what he had to say. "One of the counter people at the Chicken Shack is quitting. There's an opening right now, man. We need a replacement who can start tomorrow 'cause she's eager to go. If you want the job Kevin, you can have it."

Kevin stood there, looking shocked. Then he said slowly, "You think they'd hire me with this thing hanging over my head? Are you crazy?" Kevin's voice was shaking.

"Man, everybody knows Eddie Fry is an idiot," Jaris reasoned. "He's accused most of his employees of stealing from him. He said the banker stole from him, and he ran his wife off for taking money from his wallet. I'm the assistant manager at the Chicken Shack, and if you want the job, you got it. The pay is better than you've been getting at the pizza place, and the tips are good too."

Kevin looked like somebody who'd had the noose taken off his neck. Suddenly, he wasn't going to be hanged. He walked slowly over to a bench and sat down. He put his face in his hands, and he was breathing heavily. When he finally looked up, he spoke calmly to Jaris.

"Dude, I don't know what to say," Kevin told Jaris. "I was absolutely sure you thought I was involved in that robbery."

"No," Jaris insisted. "I'd never believe that. Not in a million years. When you were hanging with Cory Yates, I thought he'd get you into some scam, maybe a horse racing deal or something, betting on the ponies. Come on, man, I know you'd never rob some old dude like that."

"Jaris, I feel like such an idiot," Kevin admitted. "What you just offered me floored me. I can't believe it. You *know* the kind of jerk I am, and yet you'd trust me with a job where your own reputation is on the line?"

"Yeah, man," Jaris responded. "Be good if you could start right away. If you showed up for work tomorrow for the four-to-ten-thirty shift, it'd be great. We're about the same size, so you can borrow one of my Chicken Shack shirts. Neal would like to let this girl, Jenny, go right away. She's got a toddler at home and another kid on the way, and she's not feeling too good. I'll get all the paperwork done and ready for you, so just come in around three forty-five, and we're in business."

"Man, I'll be there," Kevin declared. He stood up and walked over to Jaris.

"'Thanks' seems like such a lame word, man, but thanks. You're an awesome dude. I said before that you were some arrogant jerk, and you thought you knew it all. But I guess maybe you do. I accused you of thinking you could change the world, and … you just changed mine." The two boys high fived one another. Then Jaris grabbed Kevin for a hug.

"Just one more thing," Jaris told him, his hands on Kevin's shoulders. "You lose your temper with the customers and start beating their heads with chicken legs, we're both outta jobs. In which case, I'll kill you, man. Just so you know."

Kevin laughed. He hadn't laughed in a very long time.

As Jaris watched the track practice, he felt a big load off his mind and heart. Things were back to normal between him and Kevin. Now all he had to do was make sure Kevin dealt professionally with the occasional ugly customer.

Afterward, Jaris and Kevin walked over to the Ice House for mochas.

"I remember when that pizza place where you worked was packed with customers all the time," Jaris commented. "They had this pineapple topping on the pizzas, and we all went crazy for that. Then, little by little, business dropped off. Nobody wants to go there anymore."

"Eddie Fry," Kevin stated flatly. "He bought the place and then started to cut corners. He put less cheese on the pizza, less pepperoni. He uses a lot of canned stuff—not as good as fresh. He cut back on all the stuff that makes pizza special."

Kevin sipped his mocha and then went on. "If that wasn't bad enough, Fry had ulcers. He's feeling lousy all the time, and he turned more and more of the business over to his creepy son, Jex. Eddie was always cranky and a pain to work with, but the kid was worse. What a freak. The lazy fool went to college, but he didn't learn anything. He's in his mid twenties, living off his father. He'd forget to order supplies, and we'd be serving pizzas without the right toppings. Eddie thinks the sun rises and sets on that son of his."

"Yeah, I saw Jex in there a few times," Jaris remarked. "He wasn't nice to the customers. Which reminds me, Kevin. We get some pretty nasty people sometimes at the Chicken Shack. You know, some people who might be okay under different circumstances, they get obnoxious in an eatery. The other day this older lady came in, and she said the chicken in the sandwich was grilled instead of crispy. She was so mad, she threw the sandwich at Amberlynn. Poor Amberlynn had this yucky dressing all over her chicken shirt ... *Kevin, stop laughing!*"

Kevin had laughed so suddenly, he had snorted some mocha out his nose.

Jaris continued, as serious as ever. "I'm trying to make a point here. Amberlynn, she smiles sweetly and thanks the lady who threw the sandwich at her. Get it?"

"I hear you, Jaris," Kevin replied, still chuckling. "Listen, I won't let you down, man, no way. You got no idea what this means to me. I was desperate. I help my grandparents with the money I make. I didn't know how to face them to tell them I got fired, and I couldn't even get another job. They've put out so much for me."

Kevin was now dead serious. "Jaris, you won't never be sorry about doing this for me," Kevin swore. "There won't be any temper tantrums. I'll be the biggest wimp you ever saw in your life. I don't care if they bury me in chicken wings, I'll just smile like a simpering fool. I swear it, Jaris, you won't ever regret doing this for me."

"I believe you, man," Jaris responded. "You'll do great. And you'll look good in that yellow and white chicken shirt too. Those nice big shoulders you got, perfect."

"Oh man, I always thought that was some crazy uniform," Kevin groaned. "But believe me, dude, I'll wear it proudly. Even though it's got this wacky looking rooster on the back."

"Cock-a-doodle-do!" Jaris crowed.

131

They finished their mochas and walked outside. The sun would be going down in a few hours, but now a lot of blue was still in the sky. Kevin decided to jog home, and Jaris walked over to school to get his Ford Focus.

CHAPTER EIGHT

On his way home, Jaris detoured to pass Ace's Pizza. It was still closed. Eddie Fry said he'd keep it closed until he'd gotten over the trauma of the robbery. Jaris had a strong suspicion that the pizza house would never reopen, not under Eddie Fry anyway.

Jaris noticed that Jex Fry was loading stale pizzas into the dumpster behind the store. On an impulse, he pulled into the parking lot. Jaris wasn't sure why he did that. It just burned him up that Fry would try to ruin Kevin Walker's reputation with a bald-faced lie. Jex was a tall, skinny young man with a sour expression on his face. When he saw Jaris pull in, he growled, "We're closed."

Jaris got out of his car. "I know that," Jaris replied. "The robbery, a real bad thing. How's your father doing? I've talked to Eddie a few times when I came in for pizza," he said.

"He's doing okay considering what happened," Jex answered. "This is a lousy neighborhood. Full of criminals. Pa's had a heckuva time keeping honest employees. The kids who've been working for us, they been stealing us blind. Kevin, Joey …"

"I don't know the other guy you're talking about, but Kevin Walker's my friend," Jaris interrupted. "He wouldn't take a nickel that didn't belong to him."

"Yeah?" Jex snarled. "All I know is Pa kept finding money gone. Pa could never catch anybody at it, but we figure one of the employees set up the robbery. But we can't prove anything."

"You gonna reopen soon?" Jaris asked.

"Nah!" Jex said, shaking his head and continuing to dump the rock-hard pizzas. "The robbery was the last straw in a string of bad luck. We're being hassled by the health department. Some snoop come around and found rats in the kitchen."

"Man!" Jaris gasped.

"Yeah, and we got creditors baying at our heels," Jex added. "But you can't squeeze blood out of a turnip, right? That robber got all the cash we had. Pa had emptied the safe out, and there were thousands in that night's deposit. The guy got a big haul."

"Oh brother!" Jaris groaned.

Jex tossed the last of the pizzas into the dumpster. "We'll probably file for bankruptcy," he concluded.

Jaris wished Jex good luck. He didn't mean it, but he figured why not keep the guy friendly. Jaris might want to talk with him again.

On the drive home, Jaris wondered how Eddie Fry could be so stupid as to take a night deposit worth thousands of dollars across that dark parking lot.

When Jaris got home, Mom was working on the computer and frowning. "The money for our wonderful language arts program has dried up," she complained. "We're not going to be able to implement it for the children. It's a shame too. It was so effective. We're not going to get the software we need. Everything is so messed up."

Mom looked at Jaris and asked, "Was Kevin terribly disappointed that you couldn't offer him a job at the Chicken Shack? I hope he understood the position you were in."

"No, Mom," Jaris replied. "I hired him. He starts work tomorrow. He was so grateful. I mean, the guy was so happy."

"Oh," Mom responded, a little coldly. "Well, I shouldn't be surprised. Whenever your father and I give you conflicting advice, it's no contest. You always listen to your father."

"I talked to a lot of my friends too, Mom," Jaris told her. "Some of them were against me hiring Kevin. I really debated with myself over this. I finally came down on the side of hiring him 'cause the guy really had his back to the wall."

Pop was in the easy chair, watching a football game on television. "Look at this bum here," Pop grumbled. "He makes twenty million and year, and he keeps dropping the football. Look at him—he almost fell down. What a bum. Everybody booing him, but he don't care. He gets paid anyway."

He turned his attention to his son. "So, Jaris, am I hearing right? You give the kid a job?"

"Yeah, Pop," Jaris said.

"You win again, Lorenzo," Mom griped. "I don't think I can ever remember a time when Jaris chose my opinion over yours. Yes, Jaris is risking his own reputation down there, but that's not important."

"Kevin'll do fine, poor kid," Pop assured her. "Life's kicked him around enough without his friends turnin' their backs on him."

"Oh," Mom commented, "I'm sure he'll work out superbly. He will become the best employee down there because I am *always* wrong and you are *always* right. I sometimes wonder how I could be so fortunate. I am married to a man who has the right answer to every dilemma. I must have been born under a lucky star." Mom's voice dripped with sarcasm.

Pop winked at Jaris and responded to his wife. "Monie, you were born not only under a lucky star, but under a star that showered you with beauty and brains. The question is, how could an old grease monkey win the hand of such a babe?"

The irritation faded from Mom's face, and she smiled. Pop could do it every time. Jaris smiled to himself. He hoped that he would be lucky enough to have Pop's charm when he needed it down the road.

"Jaris," Mom said, "I hope at least you made it clear to Kevin that he has to be nice to all the customers, even the horrible ones."

"Yeah, Mom," Jaris answered. "We talked about that. Kevin promised he'd toe the line. I believe him. I called Neal already and told him Jenny can quit right away 'cause I hired a guy. I told Neal this dude is a good friend of mine, and he'll fit in good. I think Neal was happy we were hiring another guy. Amberlynn is a great counter person, but one chick is enough. Like the other night when this weird-looking dude came in late, Amberlynn got really scared. I had to get her out of the front in case something happened. I think seeing two or three big guys like me and Trevor and Kevin will discourage thugs too."

"Oh, Jaris," Mom gasped, "when you tell me about strange-looking guys coming in, I get scared. I get chills. I don't like you working late at the Chicken Shack."

"It's okay, Mom. Nothing bad ever happened there," Jaris assured his mother. "We got signs telling any would-be thief that there's no more than a hundred bucks in each register, and the rest is in a safe that none of us can open. It wouldn't be worth it for some dudes to do an armed robbery for so little payoff."

"But they robbed that pizza place," Mom persisted. "How much money could they have gotten from Mr. Fry? Business there has been awful. I doubt they made more than a few hundred a day."

"I was talking to Jex, the son," Jaris explained. "He told me his father emptied out the safe to make that deposit. He said he lost thousands of dollars to the robber."

"That other guy who works there, Joey something," Pop interjected. "He comes in the garage, and he said there was like ten thousand in the night deposit. That's what Jex told him."

"Ten thousand!" Jaris gasped. "Fry must have been totally nuts to carry that much money in a bag across the parking lot at night. Man, that robber really hit the jackpot."

"It's a good thing Mr. Fry wasn't seriously hurt," Mom said. "He could have been killed."

"Yeah," Pop agreed. "This dude Joey was tellin' me the old guy walkin' his dog come along later. Fry was tied up with this here duct tape, and he was thrashing around. The old guy with the dog was shocked. He was more scared than Fry. He said Fry was pretty cool considerin' what kinda night he had, losing ten thousand bucks, getting tied up like a Thanksgivin' turkey, and left on the blacktop!"

"Kevin said Eddie Fry said he was so upset he thought he was having a heart attack," Jaris recalled.

"Not according to the old dude who found him," Pop laughed. "Fry, he's an odd duck. I never could figure a man like him owning a business. He's a miser. He cuts corners. He's a sly old dude in some ways, talkin' out of both sides of his mouth if you know what I'm sayin'. Him and his lame-brained son, quite a pair. Losers to the core."

On Tuesday, Jaris couldn't help being a little nervous about Kevin's first day on the job at the Chicken Shack. When Jaris had a big decision to make, usually his head ruled fifty percent and his heart ruled the other half. But this time his heart took over completely. He had misgivings, but Kevin was so desperately in need of help. Oliver Randall tipped the scales with his argument. Jaris had visions of Kevin insulting some old dude who didn't like the way the ranch dressing tasted. But he just drove those visions out of his mind.

Jaris came early for his shift so that he would be ready to introduce Kevin to everybody. To Jaris's surprise, Kevin was already there, wearing his yellow and white chicken shirt with the rooster on the back. Jaris wanted to laugh, but he stopped himself. He gave Kevin the papers he needed to fill in, including his Social Security number, phone numbers of close kin, and other general information. Kevin filled in the blanks quickly and moved behind the counter. Tonight it would be Jaris, Kevin, and Amberlynn holding down the fort. It was Trevor's night off, and Neal wouldn't be around for most of the night either.

"Amberlynn," Jaris said, "this is my good friend Kevin Walker. Kevin, Amberlynn Parson is a great counter person. You'll like working with her."

Amberlynn smiled. "Kevin has already told us about himself. He said he was from Texas," she commented.

"Kevin is an ace runner on the Tubman track team," Jaris told her. "He can move faster than anybody I ever saw. He's like a Texas tornado, so his mom gave him a nickname, 'Twister.' Lotta kids at school call him Twister."

Amberlynn smiled at Kevin. He was handsome. She liked him, but he didn't set off any sparks in her heart as Jaris had. It would be a long time before Amberlynn was completely over her crush on Jaris.

"Jaris tells me you're the greatest employee here," Kevin told Amberlynn. "I'll do my best, but I don't expect to displace you, girl."

Amberlynn giggled. "I try. The secret, Kevin, is don't let them get you down. No matter how unreasonable the customer is, just smile, smile, smile."

It was not long before Marko Lane and Jasmine Benson appeared. They were the last people Jaris wanted to see on Kevin's first night on the job. Kevin despised Marko, and he didn't like Jasmine much either. Whenever they crossed paths at Tubman, the insults flew. Jaris was worried that kind of behavior would spill over here, and that would be an extremely bad sign.

"I heard this rumor you were gonna be workin' here, Kevin," Marko said, seating himself at the counter, right in Kevin's face. "I couldn't believe it myself. Puttin' a mean sucka like you at a counter is like bringin' the wildest pit bull in the hood to visit your sick granny."

Kevin smiled. "I work here, you're right."

"Hey, Jaris," Marko remarked, "he stole one of your chicken shirts. I see your initials on the pocket there."

"No," Kevin explained. "Jaris let me borrow one of his shirts till I get my own."

"You used to work at the pizza place," Marko remarked. "Me and Jasmine in there last week, and we seen a rat as big as a dog runnin' across the floor."

"It wasn't *that* big," Jasmine objected, "but it was enough to ruin my appetite for pizza."

"So, what can we do for you?" Kevin asked in a cheerful voice. "We got a deal tonight on chicken wraps. Two for the price of one."

"Sounds good. Put us down for two," Marko ordered. "Hey, you know that robber who took that pizza man down. Good thing he wasn't tryin' to rob me. No robber coulda taken me down and wrapped me up in no duct tape. I'd whupped his behind. I'd o' taken his gun away from him and hit that sucka over the head with it."

"Grilled or crispy?" Kevin asked.

"What?" Marko said.

"The chicken wraps. Grilled or crispy," Kevin repeated.

"Crispy," Marko replied. A middle-aged woman and her son were standing in line beside Marko's stool. Marko turned to her and began to tell his story. "The other day I come in this house. An armed man was holding a lady and two kids and a young girl hostage. So I marched right in there and took the gun and punched his lights out."

"My goodness!" the woman exclaimed. "That's wonderful." She turned to her son who was about twelve. "Did you hear that, Damian? This young man is a hero. He saved four people from an armed criminal."

Jaris glanced at Kevin who was rolling his eyes.

"What's your name, mister?" the boy asked.

"Marko Lane," Marko answered. "I can take one of these papers out of the tray and sign my autograph for you, boy."

"Yeah!" the boy said.

Kevin started to laugh, but he quickly suppressed it. He was fighting to get into his new persona as charming wimp, and he was getting pretty good at it. "Here we go, two crispy chicken wraps. Want something to drink with that?" he asked.

"Ginger ales, supersize," Marko said.

The boy looked at the paper that Marko had autographed. "Look, Mom! Marko Lane! Thanks, mister!" The boy and his mother left with their takeout order and the autographed paper. Marko took his order and paid for it.

All this time, Jasmine had been barely holding her temper under control. "Lissen, fool," she fumed. "I can't stand much more of this. It's bad enough you shootin' off your mouth to people we know, but now you're botherin' perfect strangers. Knock it off, Marko!"

"Babe," Marko responded with an aggrieved look on his face, "I made that boy's day. He never met no real-life hero before, and he'll prize that autograph for a long time." Marko was still yakking as he followed Jasmine out the door.

Neal had arrived at the Chicken Shack, coming in as Marko was finishing his tale of heroism. "That windbag comes in here all the time," he said, nodding at the door. "Did he really do what he's talking about now? I can't imagine it really happened that way."

"Yeah," Jaris answered sadly. "It's all true. I was there. This drunken guy was holding my girlfriend and his own poor battered wife and two kids hostage. He was gonna take them all to Mexico. I called Marko 'cause he knew this guy's son, and I thought he could talk to the dude and keep him calm. Marko was supposed to just keep the guy talking till the cops came. But he was able to grab the gun and deck the bum. It was all pretty dramatic. Like it or not, Marko's a hero."

"I'll be darned!" Neal laughed. "I thought he was just telling another fish story. You never can tell about people, can you?"

Neal turned to Kevin. They shook hands, and Neal said, "Jaris really wanted you here, Kevin. I appreciate you being able to start right away. This is a pretty good place to work. I hope you stay a long time."

Neal did some paperwork, and then he took off. Jaris had the distinct feeling that he had come in to check on Kevin Walker. Maybe Neal had heard some of the rumors that Eddie Fry was spreading or other things about the hot-tempered kid from Texas. Whatever his reason for stopping by, he seemed pleased by the wide, friendly smile on Kevin's face.

"Nice to meet you, Neal," Kevin responded.

Neal glanced at Jaris, and Jaris gave a big thumbs-up.

Later in the evening, a young man came into the Chicken Shack and ordered a chicken sandwich.

"I want it extra spicy hot, man," he told Kevin.

Kevin had never seen the young man before, but there was something unsettling about him. For one thing, the guy was very nervous. Nervousness was sometimes a warning sign that trouble was coming. Often people described robbers as looking very nervous before they struck. Kevin and Amberlynn were alone at the counter. Jaris was in the back making coffee.

Jaris emerged from the back, and Kevin saw a dark look cross his face the moment he looked at the young man. Clearly, Jaris knew him.

It was Boston Blake, the first car mechanic Pop hired when he opened Spain's Auto Care.

Jaris stared at Boston Blake. He wanted to throw him out of the Chicken Shack. He wanted to yell, "You little creep, you came at my pop with a knife!" But Jaris said nothing as Kevin handed him the spicy sandwich.

"What was that all about?" Kevin asked. "You looked like you coulda killed that guy."

"He used to work for my father at the garage," Jaris explained. "The guy's name is Boston Blake. One day he was robbing the till, and Pop caught him, and the guy pulled a knife. Luckily Pop was strong enough to overcome him or who knows what woulda happened. It makes me sick to think about it."

"What's the dude doing out on the street?" Kevin asked. "That sounds like a bad rap."

"Out on bail," Jaris replied. "He's waiting for trial. He recognized me. I could tell. I came in the garage a few times when he was working there. We got along fine. I thought he was okay. Did you see how he was looking at me?"

"Couldn't miss it," Kevin answered.

CHAPTER NINE

Kevin, Jaris, and Amberlynn closed up at the end of their shift. Amberlynn's father picked her up. Jaris offered Kevin a ride home, but he wanted to jog. He insisted on getting in more running time.

Jaris clapped Kevin on the shoulder, "You were good, man. Quick, efficient, friendly. I was proud of you," he told his friend.

"I won't let you down, Jaris," Kevin promised with a lot of emotion in his voice.

Ten minutes later, Jaris locked up the Chicken Shack and headed for his Ford Focus. Before he reached his car, he saw Boston Blake leaning on the back of it. Jaris didn't go any closer. He pulled out his

cell phone and snarled, "Back off, man."
Then he yelled, "Just back off from my car,
y'hear what I'm sayin'?"

"I didn't do anything, dude," Blake
shouted back. "I just need to talk to you."

"Back off, man," Jaris repeated. Blake
didn't, and Jaris punched in nine-one-one.
"A guy out on bail on a deadly assault is ha-
rassing me at the Chicken Shack," he said,
giving his location.

In what seemed like seconds, a police
cruiser pulled into the lot, with two officers
in it. The police had been more active in the
neighborhood since the pizza store robbery.
They were hoping to catch what might be a
serial robber.

One officer approached Blake.

"I didn't do nothin'! I didn't do nothin'!"
Blake was screaming.

"That's good," the cop said, "then you
won't have any problems."

The officer checked Blake's ID and listened to his side of the story. Then he told
Blake to stay put and went to the cruiser,

probably to check for warrants. Jaris couldn't hear the whole conversation.

Meanwhile, the older cop talked with Jaris. Jaris showed his ID, explained that he worked in the Chicken Shack, and told the officer about the incident at his father's garage.

"I guess the guy's out on bail now," Jaris explained, "but as I was walking toward my car, he was leaning on it. I asked him to leave, but he wasn't movin'. I got scared."

The cops took Jaris's statement and seemed satisfied. The officers warned Blake about doing anything stupid while out on bail and told him to get going. They also told Jaris to get in his car and go home.

Jaris was shaky as he drove home. He didn't know what Blake was doing there at the Chicken Shack. He sure didn't come just to get a chicken sandwich. Maybe he wanted to talk, to try to convince Jaris to ask his father to change his statement before the trial. Or maybe he wanted Pop just to soften his version of what happened at the garage that day. Or maybe he'd come to threaten Jaris.

Jaris recalled the day that they got the terrible phone call. Twenty-year-old Blake was trying to rob the till at the garage. When Pop caught him, he pulled a knife. Jaris, Mom, and Chelsea panicked. They all imagined the horror of Pop almost getting stabbed.

As he drove home, Jaris wondered whether Boston Blake might have been the robber who attacked Eddie Fry. It was strange that the week after Blake was on the street again, the pizza place was hit.

At home, Jaris told his parents what had happened. Pop looked grim.

"I'm tellin' ya," Pop snarled, "it's a crime they let a bum like that out on the street after what he done. That he'd have the nerve to go to the restaurant where you work, boy. That worries me. You did the right thing callin' the cops. There probably wasn't nothing he did wrong, but at least the cops gonna be keepin' an eye on him."

"Won't they put him in jail now?" Chelsea asked, a tremor in her voice. "I mean, they wouldn't just let him go again, would they?"

"Well, chili pepper," Jaris responded, "what law did he break? What do they hold him on?"

Mom went to the door and made sure it was double bolted. "Jaris, what did he say to you?" she asked.

"He just said he wanted to talk," Jaris replied. "I remember once when he was working at the garage, I told him I worked at the Chicken Shack. So he knew where to find me. He waited until the place closed. When I came out, there he was by my car."

"Talk about what?" Pop growled. "What's he gotta say to you?"

"Dunno. I didn't waste time listening," Jaris answered. "I guess with the trial coming up, maybe he wants you to change your story, Pop. Attempted murder is a bad rap.

Maybe he's trying to wriggle out of it in some way."

"I hope they lock him up," Chelsea declared.

"Don't you worry about it, little girl," Pop assured his daughter.

Later, as Jaris was getting ready for bed, his father came into the room. "I need to talk to you, boy," he said quietly.

"Sure, Pop," Jaris said. Jaris sat on the edge of the bed, and Pop sat in the chair by the desk.

"How did he strike you, Jaris?" Pop asked, a strange look on his face.

"Blake?" Jaris responded. "He seemed, uh, frantic."

"Yeah, 'cause he's scared of what's gonna happen at the trial," Pop remarked. "He's lookin' at fifteen years if he gets robbery using a knife. He's maybe lookin' at spendin' the best part of his life in prison. He don't get out till he's thirty-five or something."

Pop took a deep breath. "Jaris, when I seen him at the till, I got so mad. I gave this kid a job. I trusted him. I liked him. I was thinkin' of givin' him a raise. But there he is, stealin' from me. I was like a mad bull, Jaris. I was like those bulls in the ring in Spain and places like that. Y'know, they stick those lances in them to make 'em crazy and wild. Jaris, I came at him. I was gonna whup this little thievin' punk. Maybe, y'know … maybe *I came on too strong*."

Pop was breathing hard now, and his face was contorted with anguish. "Maybe, y'know … maybe he thought I'd hurt him bad. Maybe he pulled the knife like that, to y'know, keep me at bay. Lotta young punks carry knives. It was a huntin' knife."

"Pop," Jaris protested, "he tried to stab you!"

"I don't know," Pop admitted. "Maybe he did, and maybe he didn't. I'm thinking about it. I don't remember him like stabbin' the knife at me, aiming the blade at me. He mighta just been holding it, like, defensively, y'hear what I'm sayin'?"

Jaris was surprised that his father was second-guessing himself. Pop had seemed so sure when it happened. "Pop, what's this all about?" he asked. "I mean, you said the guy pulled a knife on you and it looked like he woulda used it if you hadn't overcome him."

Pop took a deep breath. He clasped and unclasped his hands.

"I'm just thinkin'," Pop confided. "I was so mad. I musta looked like some maniac comin' at him, screamin' at him. He's a kid. This guy's like twenty. If he takes the fall for robbery with a knife, he's looking at being in the slammer till he's almost as old as me. His whole youth is gone. He might never get outta there. Look at what happened to Kevin's dad. He was locked up as a young guy, and he died inside those walls."

Pop was tormented and locked eyes with his son as he spoke. "Jaris, I gotta be sure he really meant to stick me with that blade. I can't have it on my conscience that maybe I wiped out this kids's life. Maybe he pulled that knife out of fear of what I'd do to him. I gotta be absolutely sure he meant to stab me. I gotta know if he wasn't just scared and holding the knife to protect himself from me knocking the—from me beatin' him up."

"Pop," Jaris asked, "how do you find that out?"

Pop covered his eyes with his meaty hand. Then he spoke softly. "Boy, your friend Kevin, he's been runnin' wild for a while. You been worried. He's been hangin' out with a dopester—that Cory Yates. You had the right to be pretty leery about bringin' him into the Chicken Shack. You hadda decide—do you risk your own place there or turn your back on this guy? You asked my advice, Jaris, and like a big shot, I'm tellin' you to go with your heart. Well, you did."

Pop looked up at his son. "Right after the thing happened, I told the cops Blake was tryin' to stab me when I caught him robbing the till. That's what I believed then. Now they're gonna send this kid up on my say-so. I gotta get on that witness stand and tell the jury the kid was trying to stab me to death. But now I'm not so sure. Jaris, you're almost a man. And I guess I ain't as smart as I'd like to think I am. So now I'm asking you, man to man, Jaris. What do I do?"

"Wow, Pop, I don't know what to say," Jaris gasped.

Pop took another deep breath. "I was real proud of you for what you did for Kevin. You gave him a second chance. Kevin deserved that. Maybe this punk does too. Maybe not. Look, when Blake came to work for me, he gave me the address and phone number of his parents. Waddya think if I went out there and sorta felt them out?"

"Won't they just tell you he's a great kid who made a little mistake even if he's a criminal?" Jaris asked. What Jaris had just said was the kind of thing Mom would have said to Pop. Jaris was telling Pop to be careful, don't be a fool.

"Yeah," Pop admitted, "but I'm a pretty fair judge of people. I can tell jive when I hear it. I just want to get the feel of who this kid is. I gotta do it, Jaris."

"Okay, Pop, you want some company?" Jaris asked.

Pop grinned. "Hey, I never thought you'd get around to askin'. How 'bout we go over there Saturday? I'll call 'em to set up a time." Jaris nodded okay.

"And as long as we're talking about takin' chances, boy," Pop asked, "how'd Kevin work out on his first night?"

Jaris smiled. "Better than I dreamed, Pop. He was a lamb."

On Saturday, Pop left Darnell in charge of the garage, and old Jackson offered to come around and help. Old Jackson was the former owner of the shop. He'd sold it to Pop. But Jackson wasn't enjoying retirement as much as he thought he would. He missed the garage. He missed all his cronies. He even missed Pop. "I'd rather wrestle busted beaters than listen to the old woman hassling me twenty-four-seven," Jackson remarked.

Pop had called the Blake home and asked them whether he could come by with his son and talk to them. He identified himself as Lorenzo Spain, the owner of the garage where the incident had taken place. Mr. Blake, Boston's father, seemed astonished to be getting the call. He agreed right away to the meeting.

The Blakes had a nice but not lavish home on Algonquin Street. Making their son's bail must have been a struggle. When Pop rang the bell, Mr. Blake came to the door. He looked terribly tense. He was a tall, thin man with deep circles under his eyes. Mrs. Blake sat in the living room, perched at the edge of a chair like a little bird, terribly frightened.

"This is my son, Jaris," Pop explained. "He offered to come with me today because this is a hard time for all of us."

The men sat down as Mrs. Blake went to get coffee. She put the cups on the glass-topped table in the living room.

Pop didn't know how to begin. He was trying to choose the words when Mr. Blake started speaking.

"This has been the worst nightmare of our lives. We have four children, all younger than Boston. Boston has been in trouble since his early teens. Vandalism, tagging, stealing … being rebellious."

Mrs. Blake seemed near tears as she spoke. "He never hurt anybody. He never even got in a fight. He was scared of violence. When he was bullied at school, he just took it. He told us he went to that Chicken Shack where your son works, Mr. Spain. He wanted to talk to him, but apparently your son felt threatened and called the police."

"Yeah," Jaris said, "he was waiting for me at night by my car, and I got spooked."

Mr. Blake looked at Pop. "What do you want to talk to us about?" he asked.

"Well, like we both know," Pop began, "I hired Boston to work at my garage. He was doin' great. Then I catch him robbing the till. I went in the office, and there he was helping himself to the money. I thought, 'Hey, this punk is robbing me. That's the thanks I get for hirin' him.' You know? I don't remember him saying anything. I guess I didn't give him the chance. I came at him in a rage. I was mad. I was red-hot mad."

Pop looked nervous, but he was determined to see this through. "Next thing you know, he's got this knife. I'm thinkin', 'Oh, boy, this is it. He's gonna stick me with that blade there.' I wrestle the knife from him and throw him down on the floor. He didn't put up much of a fight, I gotta say. He was babblin' about not being a thief and stuff, but I wasn't listenin'. I kept thinkin' I almost got a blade in the gut. And right now I might be bleedin' to death on the floor of the office."

"His grandfather gave Boston that knife," Mrs. Blake interjected. "Boston always carried it except when he went to school. He said it would come in handy for a lot of things. But he never would have used it against anyone, never."

"Well, you're his mother, and you're gonna say that," Pop said. "On the other hand, I got real doubts now about what went down that day. I'm thinkin' maybe the kid shouldn't be taking the rap for robbery with a knife."

Mr. and Mrs. Blake looked at one another. Both of them seemed near tears. "Mr. Spain," Mr. Blake responded, "we are so grateful that you would come here to talk to us. Thank you for even considering giving our son the benefit of the doubt. We haven't had a happy day since our boy was arrested. We put a loan on the house to bail him out. The thought of the trial coming up has been such a weight on our hearts."

"The kid told the cops he was goin' in the till just to make change from a twenty he had," Pop said. "He claimed he wasn't trying to steal from me."

Pop fell silent and looked closely at the parents. Boston was a thief. Pop had no doubt of that. But Pop wondered whether they would own that, or would they say their boy was so honest he would never steal? A lot hung on what they would say. It would tell Pop whether these people were sincere, decent people or creeps covering for their rotten kid.

Mr. Blake smiled sadly as he spoke. "That's bull, of course. He was after your money, Mr. Spain. He had a date coming up with a girl he really liked. He was trying to rob you. No doubt of that."

"He's stolen from my purse many times," Mrs. Blake added.

Pop looked at Jaris. It was an aha moment. Pop liked these people. They were stuck with a twisted kid. They were good people. They couldn't help loving this creepy kid, and they wanted to help the kid salvage his life if possible. Boston Blake wasn't yet bad to the bone. He might be sent off to some youth camp where they took guys under twenty-five years of age and worked them hard. Those places hammered it into kids' thick skulls that this was their last chance to fly right, or else the game was over and real prison waited.

"Okay," Pop declared. "Let me talk to the lawyer you got for your kid. I have some doubt that he meant to stick me with that knife. I'll change my statement with the cops. I figure there's a good chance the kid pulled the knife to defend himself against a pretty furious old dude."

The Blake parents stared disbelievingly at Pop as he spoke. "When the DA learns about this, I think they'll plea-bargain. They'll drop the felony, and the kid pleads guilty to simple theft. He wanted to lift some cash from the till, but he wasn't armed, so to speak. He'll probably have to do a year in some youth camp. But he won't be lookin' at no fifteen years in the slammer."

"Mr. Spain," Mr. Blake responded in a hoarse voice, "there are no words to express our gratitude. Thank you from the bottom of our hearts. We were in despair, but now we have hope."

Mrs. Blake was crying, but she managed to whisper, "Thank you."

As Jaris and his father headed home in the pickup truck, Jaris said, "You know, Pop, there've been lots of times when I've been proud of you."

"Yeah? Proud of the old grease monkey?" Pop asked with a rueful laugh.

"Yeah," Jaris told his father, "proud that you could take a car apart and literally put it back together. You do magic with engines. And I've been proud that you went out every day and worked like a dog for us, for me and Chelsea and Mom. Lotta my friends at school don't have a pop like that. Their fathers aren't around, and if they are around, they don't care all that much."

"You guys are my world, Jaris," Pop asserted. "No more complicated than that."

"But today, this goes beyond being proud, Pop," Jaris said. "I'm in awe. I saw how angry you were about what that guy did. When you saw him on the street the other day and figured he was walking around free after what he did, you exploded. You were spitting fire. Like you wanted this dude put in some lockup where they threw away the key. I figured it'd be fine with you if he did the whole fifteen years and then some."

Jaris paused before speaking again. "To second-guess something you felt so strongly about. To be willing to see the other side of the story, Pop, I'll never forget this. Boy, did I learn a lesson."

Pop glanced at Jaris. "You didn't need to learn that lesson, boy. You already knew it, and I think you taught me something. You hired Kevin even though, in a very dark corner of your mind—admit it— you wondered if the guy maybe did have something to do with the hit on the pizza place."

Jaris smiled. "Yeah, you're right," he agreed. "It crossed my mind, but not for long. We still don't know who did hit the pizza place. Some crook out there is thousands of bucks richer. We know that."

"Well, the cops'll get the guy," Pop said. "I know a cop down at the station. He brings his personal car into the garage when it needs work. We used to have a beer together, but now we have a cup of strong joe. He tells me stuff off the record. The cops got a lotta evidence from the duct tape Eddie Fry was bound with. They got imprints of the robber's shoes too. He had to cut across a dirt field to get to the parking lot where he made the hit. The fool left behind a lot of evidence."

Pop nodded knowingly. "The cops are sniffin' him out, all right. He was an amateur. Pretty soon the cops'll be knocking on his door. Dumb as he is, he'll probably be counting his money as they bust in." Pop laughed.

Before they got home, Jaris and his father stopped at a hamburger joint. They had supersized burgers with cheese, bacon, lettuce, tomato, and extra rich dressing.

Pop grinned at Jaris and commented, "So our Kevin turned into a lamb, eh, Jaris? A lamb!" Pop chuckled as he polished off the burger.

CHAPTER TEN

Lorenzo," Mom declared, "you never cease to amaze me. I would never in a million years have expected you to do what you did this morning. Not long ago, you were storming around in righteous indignation that that boy was roaming around free on the streets."

"Hey, as I sit here, I'm not sure I did the right thing, Monie," Pop confessed. "I am just not sure that the kid's guilty of armed robbery. I figure you gotta be darn sure before you bury a kid in prison. I didn't wanna wake up in the middle o' the night in a cold sweat and think maybe I was part of a big injustice. Having kids yourself, it makes you think like that."

"But, you know," Mom responded, "maybe Boston Blake really *is* a bad person."

"Babe, maybe he is," Pop replied. "It's a chance. A risk. It's like the benefit of the doubt, y'hear what I'm saying?"

Pop grinned at Jaris. "Like with that jerk Marko Lane. Who woulda thought that lousy punk woulda risked his own skin to go out to the Becker house and save those people? Who woulda thought that with all the mean things he's done, he'd do somethin' like that? And why did Marko go and risk his life like that? That's something he never woulda done before. He did it 'cause Jaris here and little Sereeta, they went out there and saved Marko's girlfriend Jasmine. 'Member when that creep Zendon was trying to spirit her away? They rescued Jasmine from her own stupidity.

"Get it, Monie?" Pop asked. "Life's like that. When somebody does the right thing— even though there's a risk, even though it's tough—then somebody else down the line does the right thing too."

"Yeah," Jaris agreed. "When I called Marko asking for help for Sereeta and that lady and her kids, Marko wasn't going to come through. Then I reminded him what we did for Jasmine, and that did it."

"See, babe?" Pop added. "It's all about passin' it on, payin' it forward. People have done me good turns in my life, and now I'm trying to pass it on. Much as I griped about workin' for old Jackson, he gave me first refusal on buyin' the garage. He coulda got more money than he asked me for. He coulda stuck to a higher price, and I wouldna gotten my garage. Jackson knew the place was a gold mine, and so did some other dudes. But Jackson, mean old cuss that he is, he cut me a break."

Pop leaned back in his chair, smiling.

Then Chelsea brought up a sore subject. "Pop, remember when you said I shouldn't hang with Maurice Moore? Well, we told him he shouldn't come down under the pepper trees for lunch anymore, and he doesn't. Athena said it was mean to chase Maurice, and I kinda think so too. Keisha was sorta undecided, but Inessa said we should never let him come back. Falisha said maybe. Pop, I went along with Inessa 'cause of what you said, but I want to invite Maurice back now."

"Maurice is a punk, little girl," Pop declared.

"Yeah, but now he eats by himself, and he looks so sad," Chelsea objected. "He said he wasn't going to smoke grass ever again. I see him there eating by himself, and it just makes me feel bad, Pop. Don't you think it'd be okay if he came to eat with us again? I mean, isn't that sort of what you did about that guy Boston Blake and what Jaris did with Kevin?"

"Well," Pop grumbled, "he shouldna fooled around with dope."

"But he's sorry, and he won't do it again," Chelsea persisted. "Maybe on Monday I can tell him it's okay to come eat with us under the pepper trees. I know Heston misses him because now Heston's the only guy in our group, and he feels funny. And Athena misses him. Okay, Pop?"

Pop took a deep breath. He looked at Mom. "The little girl plays me like a drum," he commented. "She's clever. She's watchin' for an openin', and we're talkin' about somethin' else, and she jumps right in there. We're sayin' take a risk and be kind to losers and stuff like that, and she jumps right in. You see that, Monie? She don't miss a trick. She's trotting out that Maurice punk when it's all nice and mellow around here."

"It's okay then, huh, Pop?" Chelsea asked. "Oh, Maurice will be so happy. It's no fun eating your lunch by yourself. Heston and Athena will be glad. I think Falisha too, and Keisha. Inessa won't like it, but that's okay. Inessa doesn't like much of anything. Thanks, Pop!"

"I didn't even say nothin' and already she's thankin' me. That's her strategy,"

Pop remarked. "Oh, she's a clever one. Okay, little girl, but the bum fools with dope again, and he's done."

Chelsea jumped up and gave Pop a hug. "I knew you'd understand," she chirped, running to her room and texting Maurice and all her other friends.

"Hear her in there?" Pop grumbled. "She's tellin' the world the news. She broke down the old man again. Got him eating outta her hand."

Mom looked at Pop. "Did you notice she didn't even *ask* me?" Mom noted. "I am so way down on the pecking order that I'm hardly visible. I have about as much authority in this house as the cat."

"We don't even have a cat," Jaris said.

"Well," Mom insisted, "if we did, the cat would have more of a say around here than I do."

Mom obviously did not want to discuss the matter any longer. She changed the subject. "Mother is coming to dinner tomorrow, and I don't want to hear anything negative from anybody. She took both you kids out for your birthdays and gave you generous gifts. The least we can do is to be civil to her. Dawna Lennox has been nice enough to make Mom's favorite casserole, and Mattie Archer made a lovely light salad. They're bringing everything over for dinner. So, Lorenzo, you won't have to bother making anything."

"Put the pork bellies and grits back in the freezer, kids," Pop bellowed. He turned to Jaris then with a grin, "Your mother's gonna pretend she made the casserole and the salad, but the old—I mean, Grandma Jessie knows better. She knows the only stuff your mom serves comes out of little cardboard boxes." Pop chuckled.

"We'll be nice, Mom," Jaris promised. "Even Chelsea. Now that we know Grandma likes Nat King Cole, that's a good subject to talk about. I bet she likes Duke Ellington too, and I know a lotta stuff about him. Another good topic for us tomorrow."

Grandma Jessie had arrived at midday on Sunday, and she was seated at the table in the Spain dining room. Dawna Lennox and Mattie Archer had barely escaped out the back door after delivering the dishes.

"Oh, my!" Grandma Jessie remarked, beaming. "Everything looks so good. What a lovely salad, so fresh and nutritious. And the chicken and green bean casserole. One of my favorites. Just delightful."

As they began to eat, they made some small talk about the new carpeting in the living room. Grandma expressed concern about spending money for new carpeting. Was it wise, she asked, to spend the money while they were still paying off the loan taken out to buy Spain's Auto Care? But then Pop mentioned that his business was up again this month.

Grandma dropped that subject and turned to a worse one. "I understand the pizza shop just down the street was robbed. Some vile criminal accosted this poor old merchant and took all his money. He was fortunate not to be murdered, as so often happens in this dreadful neighborhood."

She turned and looked at Jaris. "Dear, I hope you're safe in that Chicken Shed."

"Chicken *Shack*, Grandma," Jaris corrected her. "We got one chick, and if anything looks funny, we hustle her in the back. We got three tough-looking dudes now. Our new guy is really frightening. He'd scare off any gangbangers. Nobody wants to tangle with Kevin."

"My!" Grandma commented. "How do you know some of your coworkers aren't criminals themselves? I've seen some of the boys you hang with, Jaris. Isn't Kevin the one whose father was a murderer?"

Jaris cast Mom another critical look. Mom had shared another tale—Kevin's sad life story—with Grandma. "Yeah, Grandma, but Kevin's a great guy."

"Monica," Grandma asked, "didn't you tell me that this Kevin was an employee of the pizza place that was robbed? That would raise a red flag in my mind."

Jaris covered his eyes with his hand for a moment to regain his composure. "Grandma, Kevin had nothing to do with the robbery. He wasn't even working that night."

"All the more reason to suspect he was the culprit, dear," Grandma insisted.

"Which reminds me," Jaris mentioned, "I was going over my old musical collection of Duke Ellington songs. I like that 'Mood Indigo.' I bet that was one of your favorites too, huh, Grandma?"

"Well, dear, that was a bit before my time," Grandma replied. "He was popular when I was just a little girl."

"Yeah, well, that guy could really do jazz up right," Jaris said. "Leave it to the Duke."

"I suppose the police questioned this Kevin," Grandma persisted. "But he undoubtedly had a good alibi. They usually do. Their buddies back them up. One lies, and the others swear to it."

"Old Louis 'Satchmo' Armstrong," Pop piped up. "He was my pop's favorite. Satchmo was the king o' the trumpet. I never went for that stuff myself, but my pop loved it."

They heard a sudden racket outside. Grandma Jessie leaned forward in her chair and peered through the dining room window. "Oh, dear!" she remarked. "There are some gangbangsters out there right now, Monica."

Chelsea giggled. "Gangbangers, Grandma. They're not gangbangers. That's just Kevin and Derrick trying out Kevin's street rod."

There was alarm in Grandma's eyes. "What do they want *here*?"

"Excuse me, Grandma," Jaris said, "I'll tell them to come back later." Jaris hurried outside.

While Jaris was outside with his friends, Grandma Jessie spoke to her daughter. "Monica, those are very rough-looking boys. Are you sure they're all right? They look like thugs. One of them is wearing those horrible trousers that are too big. I understand they wear them so they can hide stolen goods in them."

"They're all right, Mom," Mom assured her. "Jaris has known Derrick—he's the one with the, uh, oversized jeans—all his life. It's a, uh, very good family."

Pop was barely holding his temper. He wasn't too happy anyway when he sat down to eat and spotted the green bean casserole and the wimpy salad. He'd been picking at his food with his head down.

Grandma craned her neck for a better view of the activity outside. "The darker one, is that Kevin?" she asked.

"The one in the black hoodie," Chelsea replied.

"Oh!" Grandma gasped. "He *is* frightening looking. Now that I've seen this one's face, the other boy looks harmless."

Chelsea giggled again. "Derrick is nice, but so is Kevin unless he's in a bad mood," she remarked. "One time, he said he wanted to rip Marko Lane's face off, but now he can't 'cause Marko's a hero. Marko went in this house where this really mean drunk was holding Sereeta and a lady and her kids hostage. He took the gun away from the guy, so now everybody has to be nice to Marko. Kevin can't talk about ripping his face off anymore."

Grandma's eyes grew very large. "Did all of this happen around here, Monica? Men with guns abusing their wives and children? And that poor troubled girl, Sereeta, in mortal danger? Monica, *what is going on*?" she gasped.

Chelsea regretted bringing the story up.

"It's all right," Mom assured her. "It didn't happen around here."

"Ohhh!" Grandma cried. "That Kevin is attacking Jaris now! Lorenzo, *do something*! He's attacking your son!" Grandma leaped up from her chair and flung the front door open, screaming. "You thugs! Leave my grandson alone!"

185

All three boys turned, froze, and stared at Grandma Jessie. Derrick looked dumbfounded until Kevin started laughing. Jaris rushed up the walk to the door. "It's okay, Grandma," he said. "Kevin's taking boxing lessons, and he was showing us how to spar and dodge."

"Kevin said he wants to be a fighter so he can pulverize bad people," Chelsea chirped.

Grandma stepped back from the door and returned to the dining room table. "This is very much like a zoo filled with dangerous wild animals." she commented in a confounded voice. "It's a whole other world from the civilized environment I am accustomed to."

"They're boys, Jessie," Pop told her. "Boys do like that. They wrestle, they spar. That's how boys have fun. You don't know nothin' about that, Jessie. You just had a sweet prissy little girl, Monica here. All she did was fix her doll's hair all day. Y'hear what I'm sayin'?"

Grandma Jessie gave Pop a dirty look and picked at the remains of her green bean casserole. The rest of the meal and dessert was eaten mostly in silence.

Pop leaned back in his chair and loosened his belt. Pop hated the green bean casserole, and he wasn't too crazy about the salad with vinegar dressing. But the apple pie was wonderful. Pop had two helpings of that. Good old Mattie Archer. She remembered Pop's apple pie.

Chelsea had excused herself and turned on the television in the living room. She was surfing the channels when came across the evening news.

"Look!" Chelsea yelled. "They got the robber who hit the pizza place!"

Everybody, including Grandma, went into the living room to hear the details unfolding on television.

"I'm so glad they caught that hoodlum," Grandma Jessie declared. "I'll bet it was one of those gangbangsters who live around here. I saw that poor man who was robbed

187

on a TV interview the other night. He said the robbery shook him up so badly he was closing the pizza place because of it."

"Actually," Jaris explained, "Mr. Fry was gonna close down anyway 'cause the health department was after him."

The on-the-scene news reporter was describing the arrest of a twenty-four-year-old man who was being led from the house in handcuffs. She was doing the voiceover for a video of the man when he was arrested.

"That's Jex Fry!" Jaris gasped. "Eddie Fry's son!"

"You mean the son robbed his own father?" Pop cried. "What a raw deal, the little creep!"

"No," Jaris said. "Listen!"

Eddie Fry himself was led out in handcuffs next. The reporter described a scheme the father and son had worked out to stage a robbery and collect a large settlement from the insurance company.

"It was all a crock!" Pop shouted. "And they had the nerve to try to blame Kevin!"

Grandma Jessie stared at the television screen. "What a terrible place this is!" she moaned. She shook her head from side to side as she took her coat off the hallway hook and started putting it on.

When Grandma Jessie was out the door, Pop declared, "And so ends another delightful family dinner at the Spain house."

Mom was glaring at them all—Pop, Jaris, and Chelsea. When Pop saw the look on her face, he did his best to stop smirking.

"I'm sorry, Monie," he said sweetly. "It's just she makes such a big deal outta nothin', honey. Everything here's dangerous. She sees bad stuff everywhere. It gets to be a little hard to take."

"All I can say," Mom declared, "is that hothead Kevin gets a second chance, and that thug Blake gets a second chance. But my mother doesn't have a chance to begin with."

Jaris stared at the TV screen, where the news service replayed the footage of the arrest and the commentators talked on and on.

"No, Mom, sorry," he thought. "Grandma has a second chance every time she comes to the house. And she blows every one of them."

But not Kevin. Kevin was in a hard place and maybe ready to do something that would ruin his life. He got a second chance to get it right. His friend Jaris gave him a job. True. But his friend Jaris gave something more important: a vote of personal confidence. Kevin had the chance now of making a better life for himself. Jaris knew he would go the right way.

Boston Blake got a break too. Pop let him off the hook. Only time would tell how Boston used his second chance. But he had good parents, and he'd probably learned his lesson.

"That's the lesson," Jaris told himself. "How you use a second chance is all up to you. Grandma Jessie doesn't get that. Kevin and Boston do."